FARM TEAM
A Billy Baggs Novel

Will Weaver

HarperTrophy®
A Division of HarperCollins*Publishers*

A Billy Baggs Novel

Harper Trophy® is a registered trademark of
HarperCollins Publishers Inc.

Farm Team
Copyright © 1995 by Will Weaver

Printed in the United States of America. For information address
HarperCollins Children's Books, a division of HarperCollins Publishers,
10 East 53rd Street, New York, NY 10022.

Library of Congress Cataloging-in-Publication Data
Weaver, Will.
Farm team / by Will Weaver.
p.   cm.
Summary: With his father in jail and his mother working full-time,
fourteen-year-old Billy Baggs finds himself in charge of running the
family farm in northern Minnesota and having to give up the thing he
loves most—baseball.
ISBN 0-06-023588-8. — ISBN 0-06-023589-6 (lib. bdg.)
ISBN 0-06-447118-7 (pbk.)
[1. Baseball—Fiction.   2. Family problems—Fiction.   3. Farm
life—Minnesota—Fiction.   4. Minnesota—Fiction.]   I. Title.
PZ7.W3623Far   1995   94-32673
[Fic]—dc20   CIP
                                                          AC

First Harper Trophy edition, 1999
❖
Visit us on the World Wide Web!
http://www.harperchildrens.com

For Roberta Ball Egersdorf

FARM TEAM

1971

Orange baseballs. A dozen orange balls flew between two lines of boys facing each other. The balls smacked into leather gloves with a continuous sound like popcorn popping. Rubber-soled shoes chirped on the maple-wood floor as the voices of eighth graders laughed and echoed in the old gymnasium.

"Get good and warm," Coach Anderson warned the boys. "You'll need it today."

There were instant groans. It was March 28 at the Flint middle school—the first day of spring baseball practice—and nobody wanted to go outside.

One boy, arriving late, stopped in the doorway. Billy Baggs was a tall, skinny farm kid with yellow hair and patched blue jeans. He stood exactly half in and half out of the gym, his blue eyes scanning the even number of boys, all paired. One of the closest boys spotted him; he pointed at Billy and whispered something to another kid. Billy's clothes were shabby and small on him.

"Billy Baggs is here—I told you he'd come!"

another voice shrilled. It was Tiny Tim Loren, the ultimate pest.

The coach looked up from his clipboard. Oswald Anderson was a round, middle-aged, bearlike man, and with the easy jog of a former athlete he trotted over to Billy. The other ball-players glanced toward Billy, then made it a point to look away. As Tim hopped up and down and waved to Billy, an orange baseball whizzed and plunked him in the ribs.

"Owwww!" Tim croaked.

The other players cracked up with laughter.

"Watch the ball all the way into your glove, Tim!" the coach called back.

Tim scuttled after the ball, clutching his ribs.

Coach Anderson arrived at the doorway. "I was wondering if I'd see you today, Billy," he said with a smile.

Billy shrugged. "Thought I'd check it out," he mumbled. Because of his crooked top teeth, which this year had begun to jut out in front, he had developed a habit of keeping his mouth mostly closed when he talked.

"Glad you did, glad you did." The coach wrote down Billy's name on his clipboard, then picked up his own glove plus one of the orange base-balls. "Come on in. Let's loosen up the old hinge."

Billy stepped through the doorway. The coach pointed to a spot, and Billy got into line.

His first toss went high over the coach's head. The ball hit with a *thunk* against the heavy curtain of the auditorium's stage; dust puffed, and a darker spot remained on the old velvet.

"Easy does it," Coach called, heading after the ball. "Loosen up first."

"If you'd been here on time, you'd be warmed up by now," King Kenwood remarked. Kenwood was the ace pitcher. He didn't look at Billy when he talked—he didn't look much at anybody when he talked. Now he continued to throw with a round, easy motion, like a deer bounding, like a trout arcing out of the water and over a dam. King was shorter than Billy but strong in the shoulders and with darker hair, and looked older. He also wore a bright new San Francisco Giants warm-up jacket. That was because his older brother was a pitcher—a real pitcher—in Triple A ball. Billy ignored Kenwood. That was his personal goal this year. Ignore King Kenwood. Otherwise there would be trouble.

After a few more tosses the coach blew his whistle. "Okay, boys, everybody outside."

"Outside? Oh man!" There were loud groans and fake sobbing noises.

"Hey—thirty degrees is better than ten below zero," the coach replied, herding them out the door.

"You wouldn't make us go outside if it was ten below!" Tim Loren said.

"Try me," the coach said.

Outside there were snowbanks. Not snowbanks all over, for Flint was in northern Minnesota, not

3

Alaska; however, where the sun didn't strike directly, there were thick, dirty piles of snow left over from the long winter. The sun was not shining at all.

Trotting, shivering, the boys crossed the street to the ball field. A few of the boys, among them King Kenwood, had put on cleats, which clattered sharply on the frozen asphalt. Billy had only his old, busted-out tennis shoes.

Arriving, they found the outfield fence buried in snow. Closer in, in short center field, withered brown grass showed through the frozen crust. The infield was bare, but the areas around the bases were frozen pools of mud. This was the freezing-thawing-freezing time of year in the upper Midwest.

"We can't play here—the field is lousy," someone muttered. It sounded like Kenwood.

"Who said that?" the coach called.

Everybody looked around; nobody snitched.

"Good. I didn't think I heard anything," the coach called. "Come on—shake a leg—spring is here, boys!"

There were more groans.

"I don't believe in gymnasium baseball, nossiree," the coach said as they inspected the frozen field. "First, you can't see the ball in the fluorescent lights. Second, baseballs are tough on the hardwood basketball floor. And third, baseball is an all-weather game, boys."

"You call this weather?" Doug Nixon muttered.

"Cold is the Minnesota advantage," the coach said to his shivering team. "It works for the Vikings, it works for the Twins, it's gonna work for the Flint Sparks, right?"

There were a few halfhearted cheers.

"Outfielders take your positions, infielders find your bases. I'm going to hit a few. Catch and throw home to Butch or King."

That was Butch Redbird, the regular catcher, and of course King Kenwood, who acted like some kind of assistant coach most of the time.

Jogging in place, hooting, their breath puffing in the chilly air, the boys lined up. Billy took a spot in right field. Tiny Tim Loren, at the end of the line, began to make snowballs and goof off.

Crack! went the coach's bat, and an orange baseball soared. Then *crack!* and *crack!* again. He kept two balls, sometimes three, in the air at a time. He drove them easily to right field, then center, then left. Racing after the ball, the outfielders skidded and slipped in the snow. The orange balls looked like Baltimore orioles—the bird, not the baseball team—trying to escape the cold weather. One ball buried itself deep in a snowbank.

"Miss the ball, you got to dig!" the coach said, laughing.

"Lucky for orange balls," someone said.

"Man, my balls are blue!" called Jake "The Fake" Robertson, who was shivering on first base.

"Watch the language—language costs you laps," Coach Anderson said automatically.

Billy got ready. *Thwack!* went the coach's bat. The ball arrowed toward Billy, a line drive that kept carrying.

And carrying.

And carrying.

Running full speed, Billy managed to knock it down. The ball ricocheted off his glove and stuck in a snowbank, where it hung like a round Christmas-tree ornament. Billy plucked it, turned and fired a frozen rope all the way to home plate—a strike to Butch Redbird. *Shakwack!* went the ball in his glove.

There was a brief silence among the outfielders.

"Geez! I wish I could throw it that far!" Tiny Tim said.

"Way to bag the runner, Baggs," Butch called, pointing to Billy as he flipped the ball to the coach, who gave Billy a smile.

Near the plate, King Kenwood was suddenly and deeply occupied with tightening the webbing on his glove.

Fielding practice continued as a light snow began to fall. At first the flakes were fine, sharp, glinting little particles, and the boys kept throwing, catching. Slowly the snow thickened to long, lazy flakes, like goose down falling from a thousand broken pillows. The boys caught huge snowflakes on their tongues and made fake baseballs;

when the coach wasn't looking, they fired them at each other. They also practiced long, hooking slides in the slippery snow. Soon, from the outfield Billy had to squint to see home plate. The coach and Butch Redbird were dim silhouettes in the slow-dancing, wavering whiteness.

"Say, Coach?" Tiny Tim finally ventured. "Did you realize it's snowing?"

"Snow? What snow?" The coach laughed and continued to smack the glowing orange baseballs to all corners of the field.

Afterward they returned to the school steaming and wet. Coach caught Billy turning away from the locker-room door. "Hey Baggs—no shower?"

"Naw. I'll get one at home."

"It's a good way to get warm," the coach said. A sharp, barny smell came from Billy Baggs.

"Hot water's free," the coach added.

Billy shrugged. "Don't need no shower."

"Any shower," the coach said; he also taught the occasional English class.

"Any shower," Billy said.

The coach changed the topic. "Listen, Billy. I wanted to talk to you about the coming season," he began, lowering his voice as the other boys passed. "I'd like to try you on the mound this year."

Billy shrugged, but a hint of smile played across his lips. Then he remembered to keep them closed over his top teeth.

"You, King and Jake. That's who I've got in mind as pitchers."

Billy listened.

"I'd be depending on you," the coach said.

Billy was silent.

"What I mean is, you've got to be here. Every practice. And on time."

Glancing down briefly, Billy nodded. "I can try," he said. "But spring planting is coming on fast—"

The coach nodded. "I know," he said, smiling. He made it a point to know a lot about the home life of each of his boys. Billy came from a dairy farm twenty miles from town, and he worked harder than any three town kids.

"And it ain't only that."

"Well what, then?" the coach asked.

"Nothin'." Billy looked down.

The coach was silent a moment. "I heard your dad is having some trouble with Randy Meyers, the used-car salesman."

"My ma's Chevy was a lemon," Billy said immediately, "and Meyers won't give her her money back."

Coach Anderson clucked his tongue sympathetically. "Don't let your dad be too hard on him," he said. He knew Billy's father, Abner Baggs, a man meaner than a Black Angus bull crossed with a junkyard dog.

Billy did not smile. "I gotta catch my ride—" he said.

"Sure, okay," the coach said. He gave Billy the thumbs-up signal. "See you next practice?"

"I'll try."

And then Billy was gone. The coach watched him go through the door and outside, where the snow was heavier now, a slanted curtain of white. Billy crossed the street and headed uptown. For a moment the tall, skinny, square-shouldered boy was silhouetted against the baseball field, and Coach Anderson had the sensation that Billy would stop and look at the field—that he would pause in the falling snow and stare at the pitcher's mound: Billy Baggs had the potential to be the best young thrower the coach had ever seen. But Billy only hunched his shoulders against the snow and hurried along, his mind filled with everything but baseball.

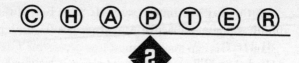
Y ou're gonna get us in trouble," Billy
Baggs said to his father. It was two weeks
after the first baseball practice, and Billy
had not been back. Too much was happening
at home.

Abner Baggs, a lean-faced, sharp-jawed man,
did not answer. He sat behind the wheel of their
logging truck and glared past Billy. The object of
his gaze was Randy Meyers A-1 Cars.

There was a little office building.

One row of used cars.

One string of bright-yellow banners flapping
above the cars.

"Yellow, like Meyers himself," Abner Baggs
muttered. The truck's big engine throbbed evenly.
Behind the cab was the low-boy trailer carrying
the yellow D–6 Caterpillar, the battered iron
monster that they used to clear land on the Baggs
farm. The Cat could move stumps, and boulders
as big as cars.

"Big trouble," Billy added. "The judge said
you ain't supposed to have any contact—"

"'Contact'?" Abner growled. "Contact is the only thing a crook like Meyers is gonna understand." His cap was jammed low across his forehead. His brown eyes traced the car lot like he was hunting big game.

"Maybe he'll still give Ma another car," Billy said. "Maybe he'll—"

Abner spat through his window and turned to Billy. "He had his chance. All fall and winter he had his chance. But spring is here."

They were silent.

"Maybe the judge—"

"The judge?" Abner said immediately, and turned to Billy. "You think Langen is going to help us?"

"I meant the law in general," Billy added quickly.

"We went to the law like we were supposed to, remember?" Abner kept his angry eyes on Billy.

Billy had no answer to that; it was true.

"First the sheriff. And what happened there?"

"Nothing," Billy had to say.

"And then that damn judge. What did he do for us?"

Billy looked down. "Nothing."

"That's right. A whole damn shitload of nothing." Abner sent a dark spurt of his chewing tobacco out his window. "Langen and his city friends."

Billy looked back to the car lot. Randy Meyers

was a crook, no doubt about it. The Chevy he had sold Billy's mother was a lemon. They had found sawdust in the transmission fluid—to keep the shifting quiet, to keep the gears from grinding. Plus the body of the car was held together by a coat of cheap paint; underneath it was all rust. The whole car was no good.

"Look—there's our man," Abner said, pointing.

Billy saw Randy Meyers pause at his picture window and look out to the highway. Billy imagined what Meyers saw: an old truck, a low-boy trailer, a battered Caterpillar. Maybe some road construction, maybe a logger, nothing new in northern Minnesota, certainly not the town of Flint. Just behind the truck was the green city-limits sign: FLINT: POPULATION 2001.

Meyers came out of his little log-cabin office, his potbelly leading the way. He was carrying a small orange sign and something else. Abner squinted and leaned forward. Meyers glanced around, then crouched beside an old green station wagon. He briefly sanded a spot of rust, shook a small paint can and gave the rust spot a quick spray. Afterward he nodded, then stood up. In the window he placed the orange sign: '69 FORD WAGON, RUST-FREE & GUARANTEED. Then he lit a cigarette and retreated to his little office.

Abner croaked once with laughter—which worried Billy still more. His father seldom laughed.

"Come on—let's go home," Billy said. "We'll get back at Meyers someday."

"Today's the day," Abner said, opening his door and letting himself down to the ground. He sounded almost cheerful now.

Billy remained in his seat. The rider's seat. He was along for the ride. In truth he had not been sure, this afternoon, when Abner had picked him up after school, where they were heading. He hadn't even known Abner was coming to get him; as Billy had headed out to catch his bus, there was his father and the long low-boy parked right in the middle of traffic. Buses were backed up behind him. Billy had climbed in without any questions. With Abner it was best not to ask.

"Help me take off the tie-downs."

"You'll go to jail," Billy said, still in his seat.

Abner shrugged.

"Both of us will go to jail."

"They don't put thirteen-year-old kids in jail."

"Fourteen," Billy said.

"Fourteen," Abner replied, loosening the chains on the Cat. Then Abner paused and looked up. They stared at each other, father and son, for a long moment. "Boy," Abner said, "you can catch a ride home if you want." There was the faintest note, a hint of understanding in his voice. "Or you can head downtown, go to the café and wait for me there. I'd understand that."

Billy looked down at his father, then at his

own face in the truck's mirror. The mirror was cracked. It gave his jaw the sharp edge of Abner's. In the split glass it was like his whole face was two different people. He didn't like looking at his face that way and turned away. "The man cheated us," Abner said.

Billy was silent.

"Cheated your mother."

Billy looked down briefly.

"Sometimes," his father said, beginning to work on the chains again, "life boils down to either goin' or stayin'."

There was silence except for the clank of steel links and the scrape of chains as his father resumed work. He stopped to look once more at Billy. "So what's it gonna be?"

Billy dropped to the ground. With a dark heart and angry hands, he helped jerk loose the last of the chains. "Stayin'," he said.

Abner and Billy slid out the heavy ramps and drove home the locking pins. Occasionally Billy looked toward Meyers's office. Randy Meyers sat with his feet up on his desk and looked out toward them. Billy's heartbeat picked up speed.

"Start the pony motor," Abner called from his seat on the Cat.

Obediently Billy scrambled atop the Cat's left track and adjusted the choke on the little engine. A pony motor was a gas motor hardly bigger than that on a lawn mower; it was there to help start the big diesel engine, especially during winter and even on cool April days like this. Billy pulled the cord. The little engine coughed alive. When it hummed smoothly, Abner reached down for the main switch and got ready. "Okay," he called to Billy.

Slowly Billy eased down the little clutch handle on the pony motor. The big engine began, stiffly, to turn over; the giant pistons, as big as Billy's legs, began to rattle and clatter as they moved up and down inside their cylinders. The trailer began to shake, and black smoke puffed skyward from the D–6's exhaust pipe.

Abner drew his hand across his throat and Billy killed the pony motor's ignition. Now the Cat's engine throbbed jerkily on its own. Abner sat back, let the engine warm. Slowly the black exhaust cleared to a clean, hot, quivering flow. Billy squinted past Abner to Meyers's office. Meyers was bent over some papers.

Abner waved Billy clear of the big steel tracks. Then, with a little steering lever in each hand, Abner drove the Caterpillar backward, tilting it down the ramp and onto the shoulder of the highway. He was smiling now.

Randy Meyers looked up briefly, then bent his head once again to his work.

Abner smoothly braked the Caterpillar sideways, then crossed the ditch and headed toward the line of used cars.

Meyers looked up.

He stared.

Then he leaned forward to stare again. Billy saw his eyes go as wide as coffee cups, and suddenly Meyers appeared in the doorway of his office.

"Hey!" he shouted.

Abner waved at him.

"Hey—what are you doing?"

Abner raised the Caterpillar's great blade.

Meyers's jaw came open, dropping with the fall of the Caterpillar's blade. Which crashed onto the roof of a '69 Ford wagon. First in the row, the Ford's roof buckled. Glass sprayed, plates of it, glinting in sunlight (which reminded Billy of wintertime, of the ice sheets he tossed from the cattle's water tank). Abner, rolling forward, used the blade to hoist the Caterpillar's nose onto the Ford—which groaned and crunched. Its tires popped—*Kapow—kapow—kapow—kapow*—and then the Cat was fully over the Ford and headed down the line of old cars.

"No!" Meyers shouted.

Abner waved again to Meyers and kept the Caterpillar rolling. One by one car roofs caved downward.

One by one their doors buckled and glass shattered.

One by one their tires popped.

Behind, him, on the highway, Billy was aware of cars screeching to a halt, of traffic stopping.

Randy Meyers ran to his office and grabbed

up the phone. Billy saw him spinning its dial, then shouting into its receiver. He came to the door, dragging the phone by its long cord. When Abner was halfway down the line of cars, Billy heard, as he had known he would, police sirens.

At the sound of the sirens Billy scrambled onto the trailer, then all the way atop the truck. He began to wave at his father, to warn him. But Abner didn't look up. He was working. The D–6 rumbled and groaned and crunched its way toward the end of the A-1 line of used cars.

The flashing red lights of the sheriff's car swooped into the lot. The Cat, nearing the end of the row, crunched a yellow Chevy Vega like a lemon under a sledgehammer.

Next to go was a shiny two-door '69 Chevy. Billy winced; it was a late model, nice-looking car. Was.

Next to go was a Ford station wagon. Glass sprayed from the windshield, and a rainbow of gasoline spewed from the rear. The whole line of cars began to smell strongly of gas.

Other sirens were loud in Billy's ears. He kept waving frantically to his father as the Flint City Police car swung into the lot. It stopped well back from Abner's D–6. Sheriff Harvey Olson stepped out of his car. Randy Meyers, racing across to the lot, shouted at him, "Stop him—it's that crazy Abner Baggs!"

The sheriff took a final draw on a cigarette and crushed it out under his boot. Then he tilted back his hat to watch. He didn't seem in any hurry. Neither did the city policeman.

"What are you waiting for? Arrest him! Look what he's doing to my cars!" Randy Meyers was hopping up and down, his potbelly bouncing. "My A-1 cars!"

"A-1, right," the sheriff said sarcastically, with a glance to the city policeman.

"You're supposed to stop him!" Meyers shouted. "Keep the peace, protect property—that's your job!"

"How would you suggest stopping a D–6 Caterpillar?" the sheriff asked.

Meyers's jaw moved rapidly, but no words came out.

"Exactly," the sheriff said.

"That Volkswagen—it's going to be a classic!" Meyers moaned, pointing. Last in the row was a blue Volkswagen Beetle. As the D–6 rolled onto it, the car squashed—*Pop!*—like a raisin under a big, steel-toed boot.

"I want that man arrested!" Meyers shouted.

The sheriff signaled to Billy's dad, who, finished with the cars, waved back. The two men knew each other. The sheriff walked forward.

But instead of stopping the Cat, Abner swung its square snout and shining blade toward Randy

Meyers's office building.

"No—" Meyers whispered.

"Whoa—hey Abner—no, not the building!" the sheriff called. He raced forward and waved both arms at Abner.

Abner tipped his old cap. "Can't hear you, Harvey," he called. He pointed to the big engine, then to his right ear.

The sheriff jumped clear of the Caterpillar as Abner plowed it squarely into the building. The structure groaned, then screeched sideways off its foundation; a water pipe snapped and sprayed, and there were sparks from electrical wires. Then the rear wall caught against the ground and the whole building began to tip.

Randy Meyers stood white-faced, frozen. He watched as his office slowly tilted, rising, rising— until it rolled with a crunching sound onto its roof. Anchored there, and cheaply built, the office was no match for the D–6. The big blade crushed through the flooring, and then the whole building burst open in a spray of yellow two-by-fours and pink fiberglass insulation.

Abner made two more passes over the office, grinding it into kindling wood. Then he shut off the Cat.

Suddenly there was silence.

A crowd had gathered by now, and flashbulbs popped. Billy Baggs remained on top of the truck.

"Afternoon, Abner," the sheriff said.

"How do, Harvey," Abner said. He remained in his seat.

"Trouble with the Cat?"

"Nope."

"Like maybe the steering hydraulics broke or something?" Billy heard the sheriff whisper something sharply to Abner.

Abner shook his head sideways. "Nope," Abner said. "I keep my equipment in good repair."

"Maybe you just lost control of it?" the sheriff said.

"I'm the best Cat skinner in Flint County, you know that, Harvey."

The sheriff sighed and tipped back his cap. "Well, don't say I didn't try to help you, Abner," he said. "You better come on down. I've got to take you downtown."

Abner complied. Down on the ground he held out his wrists. Harvey put on the handcuffs. Billy heard the click.

Then the sheriff turned and looked up at Billy atop the truck's tall cab. "You too, son."

Billy looked around.

People stared up at him. A huge pack of faces, like wolves. He was surrounded.

"I ain't coming down."

Some cameras turned his way, and the light of flashbulbs speared at his eyes. "He's the crook," Billy said, pointing at Randy Meyers.

Meyers stood dazed beside his line of crushed

cars. The crowd, silent, turned to stare at him.

"Five minutes ago I was sitting in my office doing title work on a '58 Ford," Meyers murmured. "I was sitting there having a cigarette, just doing my work. There was this Caterpillar out front, but I didn't think anything of it. . . ." As he talked, he automatically felt his shirt pocket, found a pack of cigarettes, shook one out.

"No cigarettes—" the sheriff called.

"Maybe some road construction," Meyers said, lighting a match with the same automatic motion. "What did I know?"

"No! Hold that match—" the sheriff shouted.

"Huh?" Meyers said. Abstracted, he flipped the match to the ground.

As the match touched the gas-soaked dirt, yellow flames puffed, then snaked forward into the first car. Meyers stared, wide-eyed.

"Run!" someone shouted. The crowd broke and ran like a herd of wolf-spooked cows.

There was a *whump*ing sound as the first car ignited. Then the flames began a yellow hopscotching, car to car. In less than a minute the whole line of cars was on fire. The sheriff collared Meyers and dragged him to safety.

And in the panic Billy made his escape.

He hopped down to the trailer, then the ground, and raced into the field. He ran and ran, his breath burning in his lungs, until he reached the fence. There he slipped underneath and into a Christmas-tree plantation.

It was suddenly quiet. The needles were sharp on his face but soft underfoot as he ran. Also, they left no tracks. He slowed but kept moving west, jogging, down the corridors of head-high trees. Then, when he could hear no shouting, he began to walk. The sound of a new siren made him run again, but it wailed to a stop. Only the fire truck, he knew.

At the edge of the Christmas-tree plantation he peeked out to the road. Finding it clear, he ducked across, then headed over the next field. He kept moving west, following the highway but staying out of sight, heading home.

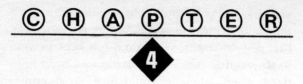

He caught a ride, the last ten miles, with a neighbor, Heather Erickson. Billy recognized the Erickson car, an old Ford, and ran toward the highway waving his arms. She braked hard.

"Jesus—what are you doing out here?" Heather called. She was sixteen and used to be pretty. Now she had a pumpkin-fat face, stringy red hair and a new baby. It was only a few weeks old, a tiny boy who lay sleeping on the seat; so far, the baby had no name. In the rear was a plastic car seat marked "Doctors' Clinic: Please Use." The infant seat held a bag of potato chips and a six-pack of Mountain Dew. But Billy could not think about Heather's problems right now. He was panting, his feet hurt and he was hungry.

"You look like shit. I wasn't going to stop," Heather said. "I thought you was some escaped convict."

"Escaped is right," Billy breathed, settling into the seat. As they drove on, he told her about Abner, about Randy Meyers's used-car lot.

"Far out!" Heather said. "I was in town and I

saw fire trucks and all kinds of burned cars. I didn't know what the hell happened. It looked like some bomb, or else a demolition derby." She turned to him. "Your old man actually did that?"

Billy nodded. A stupid grin came onto his face.

"Groovy," Heather said.

"Ga-ga," the baby went, then began to fuss.

"For Christ's sakes, are you hungry again!" Heather said.

Billy glanced down at Heather; now that she had had the baby, her chest was bigger than ever, but she had gained a lot of weight all over, too. She used to be just a neighbor kid, but suddenly she looked old and puffy, and smelled of sour milk.

"So what are you gonna do?" she asked Billy, rocking the baby sharply.

Billy looked away, down the highway. "I dunno. Go home, I guess."

As they neared the farm, he had Heather drive by once to make sure there were no police cars in the yard. There were none that he could see. Just the faded red barn, the narrow house that needed painting, the low chicken coop and sheds, plus the pale-green April grass along the south sides of buildings. In the middle of the yard, up on blocks and rusted, was the source of the current trouble—Mavis's '62 Chevy Impala. Its dark-blue paint had slipped like duck feathers molting.

"Drive in," Billy said, crouching down in the seat.

"I don't see any pigs," Heather said.

Billy looked at her, puzzled. "We've never had any pigs."

"Police. Law," Heather said, clucking her tongue as if Billy didn't know anything. As she cautiously drove into the yard, Skinner, Billy's old black Labrador, came barking and wagging his tail.

"Things look okay," Billy said, waving to Skinner but glancing around once more.

"If you need a place to crash, come over," Heather said.

"Crash?" Billy said.

"Stay. Sleep. Hide out."

"Oh, yeah," Billy said. Heather was stuck on hippie talk. She also tried to dress like one, with tie-dyed T-shirts and peace symbols and stuff, but even Billy knew that the hippie movement was dead. Still, things came late—usually several years late—to Flint, Minnesota, and Billy wasn't about to tell her. Heather was a neighbor; neighbors stuck together.

"Waaa—" went the baby.

"Shut up!" Heather said, and gave the baby a sharp shake.

Billy paused before getting out. "Um . . . how's it going? I mean with the kid."

"It's gotta go, doesn't it?" she said, as if he had asked the stupidest question in the world.

"Sure. I guess," Billy answered.

They were silent for a moment.

"Dale Schwartz—has he . . . ?" Billy began.

"I don't know what you're talking about," Heather said immediately. She set her jaw and looked off down the road.

"You know what I'm talkin' about," Billy said. "Dale—has he been botherin' you anymore?"

"Botherin' me?" Heather laughed sharply and a little crazily as she looked down at the dark-haired baby boy who was now squalling at full volume. "He bothers me six times a day."

"Dale Dale, I meant," Billy said, "not the baby."

Heather shrugged.

"I want you to tell me if he's comin' around, makin' any more threats, that sort of thing."

"There's nothing you can do if he does," Heather said, staring down at the baby. "It's me—I'm the one who has to deal with him."

After Heather was gone, Billy set about chores. He felt like he should be doing something. Some kind of work.

First things first: He climbed into the silo. His wide fork clanged once and echoed in the giant cylinder. Pigeons scuttled and flew out the top. Billy looked upward; the tall, concrete walls curved around him like a cell.

A jail cell.

Quickly he threw down heaps of corn silage, thirty rounded-up forkfuls. The silage steamed with a vinegary smell; it always smelled stronger toward the bottom of the silo, in spring. Pausing to get his breath, Billy heard pigeon wings drum and little claws scrape atop the galvanized dome. He looked up again at the concrete walls. At the little square doorway through which he had come in.

He thought again of jail cells.

Of iron bars. Quickly he threw down the last forkfuls in a great, continuous shower. And afterward, in the only fun part of silo work, he let himself plop down several feet onto the soft, smoking pile of corn.

In the barn, Billy pushed the silage cart with its rounded-up heap of smoking, chopped corn along the feed alley. The cows, locked in their stanchions, strained their necks forward. Billy slung a large forkful of silage to each one. Then he followed with a smaller cartful of ground feed, a white, floury mixture of corn, oats and salt. It was ground at the Feedmill in Flint.

Usually Billy knew just how much ground feed to give the Holsteins. Cows that had just calved and were milking heavily got a full shovelful. Those cows whose calves were older, and who were nearly dry of milk, got only a sprinkle of grain. But today he slung meal toward the cows without measuring.

Except for Stretchy, his favorite cow.

She was named Stretchy because she always leaned way back and pooped beyond the gutter, which made a large mess in the center alley. She was also by far the friendliest cow in the barn. Today, as usual, she mooed loudly and curled her thick pink tongue toward Billy. She was old, and didn't milk worth a damn these days, but she always gave Billy a wide, yellow-toothed smile. He paused, took a brief look around, then gave her a full shovel of grain. Who was to know?

In the milk house he fit the parts of the Surge stainless-steel milking machine together. There was the kettle. The lid. The rubber gasket. The four little air hoses. The four teat cups. He did this automatically, looking out the little window and down the road. No one. No cars. His mother, Mavis, would be home from work in a couple of hours (she had to ride, once again, with their neighbor, Mrs. Pederson). He kept wondering where his father was now. At the police station, no doubt. He wondered if Mavis was there with him. She would probably bail him out, bring him home.

And Billy knew what he had to do. It was early, but he had the feeling he had best get the milking out of the way. He turned on the air compressor and lugged the milker and wash bucket into the barn.

By the twelfth cow Billy was sleepy. The warm flanks of the cows made good cushions to lean his head on, and the *chucka-chucka-chucka* of the milker set up a rhythm, a rhythm like he was on a large ship. The cows were two long rows of oarsmen, and the whole barn was moving steadily forward . . . the sun was shining . . . far off a sea-gull was barking and barking—

"Billy?"

He jerked upright on his milking stool. His mother's voice. But also a jingling sound behind her, and the sharp smell of cigarettes. Neither of his parents smoked. He peeked over the spine of the Holstein. There stood his mother, Coach Anderson and a deputy sheriff.

All looked at him. Billy's eyes darted left and right. He was trapped among the cows.

"Relax, Billy, nothing's going to happen to you," Mavis said. Her eyes were red; she'd been crying.

"Hey, Billy," Coach Anderson said.

"Coach."

"This is Deputy Sheriff Porter. He needs to ask you a few questions, Billy," Mavis said.

"About what?" He turned back to the cow, to the milker that was beginning to draw air. Expertly Billy shucked off the four teat cups, poured a white flow into the milk can, then swung the milker to the next cow.

"You know what," Mavis said.

"Were you in town today?" the deputy began.

"Sure," Billy said. "I'm in town every day. At school."

The deputy narrowed his eyes. "You know what I'm referring to," he said. "Your father and his Caterpillar and Randy Meyers's car lot."

"What about it?" Billy said.

"You were with him, right?" the deputy said, "at Meyers's car lot?"

Billy was silent.

"He picked you up after school with the truck and the Caterpillar, right?" the deputy said. "That's what several witnesses at school said."

"Who said?" Billy said angrily. Snitches. Some snitch was going to pay.

"It doesn't matter who," the deputy said.

"Billy," Mavis said, half angry, half pleading, "be helpful."

"Okay, I was with him," Billy muttered.

"Did you assist him in destroying the Meyers car lot?"

"What do you mean by assist?" the coach said, stepping forward. "Look—if this is some kind of interrogation, doesn't he have some legal rights? If adults have Miranda rights, don't kids have some equivalent?"

The deputy glared at the coach. "Adults have Miranda rights and kids speak when they're spoken to."

The coach narrowed his eyes and held his ground.

"Okay, okay," the deputy said, backing off. "But substantial property was destroyed. I just want to know if he assisted his father."

"Yes," Billy said suddenly. "I helped him every damn way I could."

Mavis looked down.

The deputy turned to the coach, then to Billy. "Son, you're going to have to ride into town with me and answer some more questions."

"Now wait a minute—" the coach said.

"We've got a juvenile counselor there," the deputy said, "and—"

"Where's my old man?" Billy said suddenly.

There was silence.

Mavis's forehead furrowed to a frown. "Your *father* is in jail, Billy," she said.

"For how long?"

"Not long," the deputy said. "For now."

"So who's going to milk these cows," Billy said to the deputy, "you?"

"Don't get smart with me, kid," the deputy said, stepping forward.

"He has a point," Coach Anderson interjected. "Tell you what, Deputy. Let Billy finish his milking. I'll stay here with him, then I'll bring him to town myself. We'll be there by five thirty."

The deputy looked skeptically at the coach.

"I'm his coach and a friend of the family," Coach Anderson added. "I'll vouch for him."

"Okay," the deputy said dubiously. He flapped shut his little notebook. "But we'll expect to see him this afternoon at the police station no later than"—he checked his watch—"five o'clock."

Mavis nodded, and then the deputy turned to leave. He glanced at the cows on either side and stepped carefully along the alleyway—but not carefully enough. Stretchy swiveled her neck to stare at the stranger in the barn; then she humped her back. Billy's eyes widened; he knew what that meant. Stretchy let fly a smoking stream of dung. The deputy shouted and jumped, but he was not quick enough. The brown stream caught him squarely on the side of his leg.

"Shit!" he shouted. He tried to jump again, but slipped and went down on one hand. The hand went squarely into the steaming pile. The deputy swore again as he straightened up, holding his dripping hand at arm's length.

"I'm very sorry," Mavis said, though she did not sound all that sincere.

The deputy glared at her, at the coach and Billy.

"There's a water hose just outside," Mavis added, covering her mouth, where a smile was forming.

The deputy spun on his heel and headed out. There were squishing sounds in his shoes. Coach Anderson began to wheeze with laughter; he bent over but couldn't hold back great belly laughs.

Mavis laughed out loud, and even Billy managed a grin.

After chores, Mavis made Billy wash up and put on good clothes.

"Clean clothes to go to jail?" Billy said.

"You're not going to jail," the coach said, "just to the station to answer some questions. And your mother's right. It's important to make a good impression."

Billy stepped loudly upstairs. Behind him he heard Mavis and Coach Anderson talking. She thanked him for all his help.

"No problem," he said. "I'm glad you called me. I wish more parents would."

Leaving for town, Billy rode with the coach in his little Toyota. Mavis had seemed to want him to ride with the coach, but she drove close behind in the farm pickup—real close, as if to keep Billy in sight. As Skinner's barking faded away behind, Billy looked back toward the farm.

"Don't worry," the coach said. "You'll be back in no time."

Billy turned to face the road. They drove on for a while. Neither of them said anything.

The coach reached under his seat, found a small packet of Rum-Soaked Crookettes cigars. He rustled off the cellophane wrapper and lit one. "A secret bad habit of mine," he said.

Billy smiled a little.

The coach puffed away, and Billy relaxed some in the smell of tobacco.

The coach looked at the gray, passing fields. "Spring planting is coming up fast," he remarked.

"Still too wet," Billy said. "'Nother week or so, maybe."

The coach glanced over to Billy.

"Your father might end up with some jail time."

Billy was silent. He stared down the road.

"He was not the most cooperative guy at the sheriff's office," the coach added.

Billy nodded.

"But he'll be out on bail tonight," the coach said. Billy could tell he was trying to be cheerful.

"How much bail do you think?"

"It depends on the county attorney and Judge Langen."

"Langen?" Billy said quickly. "Langen can't make him pay." For an instant he thought not of the judge but of his daughter, Suzy, the tall blonde eighth grader who appeared regularly in Billy's dreams.

"Langen? Why not?" the coach asked.

Billy looked away, and his mind returned to the moment. "My old man and him go back a ways."

The coach glanced over at Billy, then turned his attention back to the road. They kept driving. "Well, after your father's bailed out," the coach continued, "he'll be home for a while, a few weeks, say, and there'll eventually be a court date."

Billy spit out the window. "He won't pay bail."

The coach ignored that. "And Judge Langen will probably fine him."

Billy looked again to the coach. "He won't pay that, either."

"Or give him some jail time, or a combination of the two," the coach finished.

"Not a damn dime," Billy added, setting his face toward the highway, "not to Langen."

"So what's the bad blood between your father and Langen?" the coach asked.

"It's a long story," Billy said. He turned his face to the fields.

The coach drove on, silently, and waited.

"It goes back to when my brother was killed."

"Robert," the coach said softly.

Billy looked briefly at the coach.

"At the end of last summer I went back through the old newspapers and read up on it. I remembered the tractor accident but didn't know you or your family then," the coach said.

Billy swallowed and looked away again.

"I do remember that Langen was county attorney at the time. Didn't he make a big deal about the need for more laws on farm safety, something like that?" the coach added.

"I dunno." Billy kept staring off across the fields.

"And got himself elected judge?"

Billy wouldn't say any more, and the coach let it drop. They drove on for a spell, the coach's lips squeaking as he puffed on his cigar. "Anyway, my guess is that your dad will get a fine and thirty days or so in jail. No more than that," he said. "Everybody knows that Meyers is a crook and a cheat. That's why he had his car lot just outside the city limits."

"Lotta good that done him," Billy said.

"Did him," the coach said.

"You shoulda seen them cars crunch," Billy said, turning to the coach.

"Those cars."

"And Meyers running around like a fat old rooster with his head lopped off."

Coach Anderson, behind his cloud of cigar smoke, fought back a grin.

"And then Meyers himself setting things on fire," Billy said. "It was worth every day my old man has to spend in jail."

The coach's smile slipped away. "I hope you're right, Billy," he said. "I sure hope you're right."

At the courthouse steps things were no longer funny. Billy hung back, but the coach and Mavis were on either side of him. He got the idea that if he bolted, they would snag him in a second.

Inside there was a counter, and above it a grill-work of metal bars. Mavis and the coach had to speak through a round iron hoop just big enough to pass papers back and forth. A radio squawked in the background, and there were wanted posters on the walls, the same kind as in the post office. While he waited, Billy read the names of various criminals, their descriptions. Nearly all of them had tattoos.

Suddenly a low-slung, chunky woman younger than Mavis, dressed in a plain skirt and white blouse, came through a side door. "I'm Mrs. Anne Sanders," she said, smiling at Billy like it was his lucky day. She didn't even have on a police uniform. That was because she was clearly a plainclothes officer—probably FBI or Secret Service, Billy guessed.

"Won't you come this way?" she said to Billy.

Billy swallowed. He felt the coach's big hand on his back. Into the office they went.

"Have a seat, Billy," the woman said.

Billy sat. Behind her was a long mirror, a funny yellowish kind of glass, that covered all one side of the office. For a second Billy thought he heard voices behind it.

She took a long time rustling through some papers, looking at them. Finally she looked up, smiled and said, "Full name?"

"I ain't going to rat on my dad," Billy blurted.

The woman smiled. "Don't be nervous, Billy. It's you we're here to talk about, not your father."

Billy clammed up.

"His name is William J. Baggs," Mavis said.

"The J is for?" the woman inquired.

"Jefferson."

"Thank you," the woman said, keeping an eye on Billy. She wrote that down, then set aside her pencil, leaned back. "Maybe I should tell you about myself first." And she began to talk. About her husband. About her family. Billy was surprised to hear that she had two kids in elementary school. That she actually lived in Flint.

"You ain't from the FBI?" Billy asked.

"No, Billy, not at all," Mrs. Sanders said. "I'm with the Flint County Social Services. You might think of me as a kind of bridge between families and law enforcement. A counselor."

Billy was silent. He felt some better.

And her questions were not all that bad. They weren't about bulldozing Randy Meyers's line of cars. They were about him. About the farm. About what kind of house they had. If he had his own room. If there was running water.

"Of course we have running water," Mavis interjected.

"It's okay," the coach said easily to Mavis. "She's just getting some home background data. It's important information," he added. "At school it often explains a lot about kids, their behavior."

Mavis was silent but arched one eyebrow.

The counselor asked Billy what he did for fun. He told her about swimming, about shooting striped gophers. Then she asked how much work he did on the farm. He proudly listed his chores. She kept writing and writing. Her pen made tiny scraping noises on the paper. Suddenly he got the feeling he should stop.

"Stuff like that," he finished lamely.

"Milking, barn cleaning, silo filling, haying, plowing—to name just a few. That's quite a list for a fourteen-year-old," the counselor said.

Billy shrugged. He had left out fencing, wood-cutting, corn picking, winter trap lines and about a hundred more.

But the woman kept smiling and turned her questions back to the fun things. She asked about pets. Billy told her about Skinner—he had forgotten Skinner—and some of the things they did together.

Then, still smiling, she said, "When you get in trouble, does your dad ever strike you?"

The last question came at Billy like a fastball. He was used to her slow, fat pitches, and then, out of nowhere, the fastball.

"Strike me?"

"Hit you." She kept her smile even.

"Well—sure," Billy said. He should have looked at Mavis and the coach: His mother was trying to tell him something with her face, with her eyes; the coach was giving hand signals as if this were a close game going into the ninth inning, bases loaded.

"Like when?" she pressed.

"Well," Billy said, "once I sneaked out his deer rifle to shoot gophers with. There was a ricochet and I killed a steer. He whaled on me good, that day."

"'Whaled' on you?"

"Whupped me."

"Whipped you?"

"Sure," Billy said.

"Not with a whip," the social worker said; she leaned back slightly.

"Naw," Billy said. "With his belt."

She stared at Billy, then rapidly wrote something on her piece of paper.

"So let's talk about today," she said, her smile back in place.

Billy drew back slightly in his chair. He was beginning not to trust someone who smiled so much.

"Did you want to go along with your father to Meyers's car lot?" she asked. "Or did he make you go?"

Billy paused. He looked at Mavis. She had told him, always, to just tell the truth and things would work out. So he did. "I didn't know where we was going at first," Billy said. "I was just along for the ride." To the side he saw the coach nodding.

"After you knew what your father had in mind, did you say anything to him?" the counselor asked.

"I told him he was gonna get us in trouble." The coach was nodding faster now, smiling encouragingly at Billy.

"What was his reply?"

"That I could leave if I wanted."

"And you said?"

"I said I was stayin'," Billy said.

The woman wrote this down. "And why did you want to stay?"

"Because Meyers is a crook."

"Isn't that for the law to decide?"

"My old man says that the law don't work the same for everybody, especially for country and poor people. That sometimes you have to give the law a good kick in the ass to wake it up."

The coach slapped a hand to his forehead and groaned slightly.

Mavis looked down.

The counselor kept writing for a long while. Finally she said to Billy, "That's all for now. But I'll need to speak with your mother. Alone."

The coach waited with Billy outside the office. Soon enough Mavis came out.

"Is everything all right?" the coach asked her. Billy stared. Mavis was white in the face and her look was part angry, part scared.

"The social worker said she'll have to do a home visit—a 'home evaluation' she called it."

"Routine," the coach said, waving a hand. "Just part of the paper shuffle. They have to make it look like they're working."

But Mavis's frown did not leave her. She stared back at the social worker's office, at the closed door. In the hallway the three of them just stood there; no one seemed to know what was next. The coach took charge. "Why doesn't Billy come with me while you visit your husband," he said to Mavis.

"Thank you. That's very kind," Mavis murmured, and turned away to the jail.

"Come, Billy, we've got things to do," the coach said.

They passed down several halls. Smoky paintings of old men hung on the walls, and the wooden floors were creaky and uneven with age. Suddenly they stood outside an office door that had MARK KENWOOD, COUNTY ATTORNEY stenciled across cloudy glass. Billy looked uncertainly at the coach. "Buck up," the coach said. "In baseball, as in life, sometimes you have to make a good pitch." With that he caught Billy by the back of his shirt and steered him inside.

Mark Kenwood, a middle-sized man with fashionably long sideburns and a paisley tie, was speaking into a hand-held tape recorder; he glanced up and kept dictating as he gestured for the coach and Billy to take a chair. They remained standing. Kenwood finished his letter, something about someone needing a building permit, and he clicked off the machine. "Good afternoon, Coach. And . . ." His eyes fell on Billy.

"Billy Baggs." The coach, still gripping Billy's shirt, hoisted him slightly higher; Billy nodded once to Kenwood.

"So it is," Kenwood said evenly. There was

silence for a moment. "And to what—if I couldn't guess—do I owe the pleasure of this visit?"

"The Abner Baggs case," Coach Anderson began.

Kenwood glanced again to Billy, then back to the coach. "Though I pride myself on never being a sucker for emotional appeal, it would be easier to talk without young Billy here."

"True," the coach said. "But you and I are friends, and Billy here just wanted to know what kind of trouble his father is in. Wanted to hear it from the horse's mouth."

"I did?" Billy said.

The coach tightened his grip on Billy's shirt.

Kenwood shrugged. "Bad news, kid," he said, picking up a heavy folder, then letting it drop with a *thud*.

"How bad?" the coach interjected.

"We're talking serious numbers here," Attorney Kenwood said. "Property damage of at least twenty thousand dollars—which gets us well into the felony range."

"Twenty thousand? For a dozen old junkers!" Billy exclaimed. The coach kicked him in the back of his leg.

"Blue-book prices, kid," the attorney said, "and don't forget his office that your old man bulldozed into toothpicks."

There was brief silence. "Mark, everybody knows Meyers was a crook," the coach said.

Kenwood replied, "Remind me to excuse you

from jury duty." He smiled but the coach didn't.

"I don't care about Meyers one way or another. We just want to know how things look for Billy's father."

"Not good," Kenwood said. "I'll have to throw the book at him. People—even in Flint County—can't go around flattening car lots with a D–6 Caterpillar."

The coach paused. "You said jury duty. Will there be a trial?"

"I doubt it," Kenwood said. "Abner Baggs freely admits his guilt. And the newspaper has the whole thing recorded—have you seen the new *Newspoint*?" He looked squarely at Billy this time and pushed a newspaper across the desk. The coach and Billy stared down at the front-page photograph.

FATHER AND SON DESTROY CAR LOT, Billy read silently.

"Damn," the coach murmured. Billy looked at himself in the picture. Perched atop the cab of the truck, he looked like he was a movie director in charge of the whole scene—a battle scene where no cars had survived.

"There'll be a hearing and then the sentence," Kenwood said.

The coach looked up quickly. "Sentence? What kind?"

Kenwood tipped back in his chair. "First tell me why you're so interested in Abner Baggs."

The coach was silent. Finally he cleared his

throat and spoke. "It's not so much Abner as Billy here."

"Billy the ballplayer."

Coach Anderson nodded.

"Kid has it tough? Is that it?" Kenwood asked, staring straight at Billy now, who stared back.

"That's right. And it would be a lot tougher with his father in jail."

Kenwood's chair squeaked again. "I appreciate what you're up to, Coach, but we have a felony charge here. I'll have to ask for restitution plus a year in jail."

"A year in jail!"

"My hands are tied, Coach."

"Restitution, paying for damages, that I can see. But a year in jail—Abner Baggs has a farm, a dairy farm."

"It's not as bad as it sounds," Kenwood said. "The judge will likely suspend most of it—depending on how quickly Baggs pays Meyers for his cars. He probably will end up with thirty days, and probation for the rest."

"But even thirty days. With the wait for the court date, that's a good part of the summer, and summer is when the majority of the work has to be done on a farm. Plus I'm thinking of the baseball team. With King and Billy on the mound—"

"Well, maybe Billy will have to stay home one more summer and milk the cows."

There was a long moment of silence during

which Billy glared at Kenwood.

"Hey—I'm just doing my job," Kenwood said, turning to the coach.

"Sure," Coach Anderson said sarcastically. "One last question: How much is bail for Abner Baggs?"

"I recommended five hundred, and the judge agreed. Sorry, kid," Kenwood added.

Billy said something unprintable to the man, words that reddened Kenwood's cheeks as if they had been branded by two hot pokers. "Coach, you'd better get that kid out of here or I'll put him in the same cell with his father!"

"We were just leaving," the coach said, propelling Billy toward the door.

Outside in the hallway they stood for a moment. Coach looked down at Billy. "Oh well," he said, mustering part of a grin, "it was worth a shot."

Suddenly Kenwood stepped out into the hallway. He appeared not to see Billy at all. "By the way, Coach," he said, his voice completely friendly this time, as if he had switched to a different radio station, "I've been meaning to ask. Do you think King is old enough to add a forkball to his pitching repertoire? He's in such good condition, such a mature kid, I think he's ready. What do you think?"

The coach glanced down at his own watch. "Gotta run, Mark," he said. "We'll talk sometime."

"Stay in touch!" Kenwood said pleasantly.

The coach himself muttered something unprintable and scattered people as he stalked down the hallway. "A forkball at age fourteen," he said to Billy. "Just what I need, King throwing forkballs and you stuck on the farm this summer."

Billy zipped his lip and followed. The coach turned into the Clerk of Court's office and went to the counter, where he spoke with a pale man who wore half glasses.

"Abner Baggs, yes," said the clerk, and slid forward some papers for the coach to sign. The coach also pulled out his checkbook, paused a moment, then scribbled out a check. The clerk thumped the papers one by one with a round rubber stamp, then picked up the telephone. He spoke briefly, then turned to Billy and the coach, gave them a narrow, fishy smile. "He's all yours."

In parting, behind the coach's back, Billy gave the clerk a flying middle finger.

As they headed to the jail, Billy spoke up. "Pa ain't gonna be happy with what you did. Paying his bail."

"How's he gonna know?" the coach said, arching one eyebrow at Billy.

"He don't like owing anybody anything."

"Your father doesn't owe me money. I'll get it all back when he appears before the judge for his hearing."

"Still, he owes you a favor," Billy said stubbornly.

"I'll work that out with him," the coach said.

"Right now I'm late for supper." And with that he slipped out the side door and was gone.

Billy waited alone in the jail lobby. He listened to the sounds from deeper inside the cell block. A man coughed continually; two other men argued; someone kept rattling something tinny across the iron bars.

Soon enough there was the clang of steel doors, and the sound of his father's voice. Billy jumped to his feet. "Well, somebody sure as hell paid bail," Abner said.

"It wasn't me," Mavis retorted.

"Keep it down, you two," the jailor said. "You can argue out on the street."

Abner appeared in the doorway. A tall man, tilted to the right from his polio limp, he stopped short to stare at Billy. For an instant Billy thought his father was going to reach out to him—take him in his arms.

"Last time I saw you, you were hightailin' it over a fence."

Billy froze.

"Leavin' your old man in the lurch like that—what kind of son are you? I ought to whup your ass."

Billy looked down, then back up, and felt something inside his chest harden like a fist.

t home, with a lot of silence in the house, they all went to bed early. Come morning Billy made sure he was in the barn and feeding silage well before his father arrived. He watched from the corners of his eyes as Abner surveyed the gutters (empty) and hay mangers (full).

"Well, things look pretty decent around here, I guess," Abner said evenly.

Billy let out a breath and slowed his shoveling. When Abner went into the milk house to ready the milker, Billy sneaked Stretchy her usual extra shovelful of grain.

During milking, when the rhythm of the barn thumped its slow, steady beat, Billy edged near his father. He wanted to ask Abner what it was like in jail, but didn't. Silence usually worked best with Abner. Silence and good work.

This morning Billy made sure to stay exactly one cow ahead of the milker. His job was to wash teats: splash the udders with warm, chlorinated water, then strip out a squirt of milk from each of the four pink teats. This sanitized and stimulated the udder—made the cow "let down" her milk in preparation for the milking machine.

"I heard the deputy was out here."

Billy nodded.

"I heard he had some bad luck in the barn."

Billy told Abner about Stretchy and the deputy. His father's face slowly softened, loosened; finally he laughed out loud—a croaking, rusty laugh that sounded like an injured crow. That was because Abner never laughed much. Stretchy stood within reach, and Billy watched his father give the old cow a brief knuckle rub along her spine, something every cow loved. "Right on his leg," Abner repeated, and croaked again.

Billy smiled. He wondered what he himself sounded like, laughing—probably just like his father. He moved on to the next cow.

"That's it?" Abner said at length to Stretchy. He hefted high the milker; milk splashed faintly inside.

Stretchy curled her big head around and gave a yellow-toothed "Moo!"

"Shittin' on the deputy or not, you better start doing more than moo at me," Abner muttered as he poured no more than a quart into the pail, "or else you're headed to South Saint Paul."

"She must be off her feed," Billy said quickly. "She milked fine yesterday."

After chores Billy and his father headed to the house. The sunrise was pale pink, pale orange, pale yellow—a new day on the Baggs farm. The roosters crowed and Skinner raced. From the safety of the haymow door a row of orange barn cats, full of milk and dull as pumpkins, squinted down sleepily at the goings-on. Abner paused to look once around the farmyard. "Damn good to be home," he said.

Billy picked up a corncob and pitched it high for Skinner. Abner watched as Skinner raced off and snatched the cob from the air. It was a trick Billy had taught him. "That old dog's got good bloodlines," Abner said. "A little training, he could be one of those champion retrievers."

"You think so?" Billy said excitedly.

"Hell, yes," Abner said.

At breakfast Abner's pleasant mood continued. "These flapjacks sure beat jail grub," he said to Mavis. "One meal was enough for me."

"I should hope so," she replied, arching one eyebrow as she passed the plate around.

Abner winked at Billy. Billy smiled behind a giant forkful of flapjack. He knew his mother was still very angry about the trouble Abner had caused.

Abner looked through the window to the sky, which was lifting to light blue. "We might even give the grain drill a try today. Maybe it's dry enough to plant oats—what do you think, Billy?"

Billy. His father seldom used his actual name, and Billy looked up from his pancakes, surprised.

"I think it'll go," he said quickly. "There's been a breeze."

His father nodded and bent low to finish his cakes.

Billy did, too.

They ate noisily and fast.

Mavis paused to watch them. "You know," she said slowly, "it seems to me there are two types of people in the world. There are people who lift their forks to their mouths, and there are people who dip their heads to their plates."

Billy and Abner paused to look up at her.

"I'm talking table manners here," she added.

"How you eat depends on how you was raised," Abner said.

"Exactly," Mavis replied, glancing from Abner to Billy, and arching one eyebrow again.

Abner and Billy stared at each other. Then Abner bent low to his cakes, but Billy tried to sit up straighter. It was a fine line to walk, being the son of two different people, and when they weren't looking, he stared for long moments at both his mother and his father. He fantasized briefly about trading Abner and Mavis for another set of parents. Perfect parents. Trouble was, he couldn't think of any.

CHAPTER

7

Monday after school the coach was surprised to see Billy at baseball practice, and right on time at that.

"Coach?" Billy said.

"Hey, Billy!" the coach replied.

Billy paused as if he had something to say.

Several boys jerked their heads Billy's way and whispered behind their gloves.

"What is it?" the coach asked.

"Ah . . . nothing."

"Well, if it's nothing, let's jog a few laps," the coach said. The boys groaned and tossed their gloves along the wall. Billy joined the end of the trotting caravan of boys.

Tiny Tim attached himself to Billy. "I thought you were in jail," he said excitedly.

"Was—" Billy said. Which was not really a lie. Ahead some town kids snickered. "But I'm out now," he added, louder, and some space opened up between him and the town boys. Dusty Streeter and Butch Redbird cruised up. Butch smelled of cigarettes.

"Way to make the headlines, Baggs."

Billy held back a grin.

"Top-notch photo," agreed Dusty, "except that you looked like a hood ornament."

"He is," said Tiny Tim. "Hood ornament—get it?"

"Watch it, pip-squeak," Butch said.

Tiny Tim grinned and kept running near Billy's group, though just out of arm's reach.

Jake the Fake loped up. "Dang it, Baggs—I was going to steal the bucket seats out of that '69 Chevy. Now it's flatter than road kill!"

When they realized Jake was seriously put out, the group went stumblebum with laughter. All except Billy. He looked once over his shoulder toward the coach, who was watching. King Kenwood and Nix Nixon led the other players who were not goofing off. Kenwood's group was mainly the lawyers' and dentists' kids, most of whom lived in Green Lawn, a development of newer rambler homes that was Flint's only suburb. Between the two clusters of boys there had developed a major gap.

"Close it up," the coach shouted. He sounded angry. "One line. Close it up!"

After warm-up they went outside. The temperature was a spring-training high of fifty degrees. The sun shone and the pitchers got to throw their first batting practice.

"Just throw strikes," Coach Anderson called.

Kenwood took the mound first. He threw smoothly, with a wheeling, full follow-through that grooved the ball at half speed. The batters were not as sharp. Dusty managed to hack two grounders. Tiny Tim struck out on three pitches. Two more batters hit mainly fouls. And then it was Billy's turn.

Billy took some practice cuts, then stepped into the batter's box.

"Helmet—" the coach called.

Billy quickly stepped out for a helmet, then got ready again. His arms felt loose and ready. That was because swinging a bat was not unlike swinging an axe, a shovel, or a silage fork, something he did every day of his life.

He mashed the first pitch down the third base line into the corner.

He drove the second pitch deep to left field, where it ricocheted off the wall like a bumblebee off a windshield.

Butch Redbird gave a brief yodel, and Kenwood turned away and rubbed up a ball. Kenwood readied himself, then threw Billy his third pitch.

Billy knew King would try something. And sure enough, the ball came in knee high and very fast—Kenwood's best heater. Billy almost didn't get around on it. But he dipped his back knee and golfed at it.

Crack! The ball scorched over second base, kept rising and curving into left field, where it cleared the fence with twenty feet to spare.

"Nice opposite-field stroke," the coach called.

Kenwood glared at Billy. As Billy loped with

his glove toward the outfield, Kenwood said softly, "Three months." He spoke without looking at Billy. No one else could hear him.

Billy stopped.

"My dad says a minimum of three months in jail."

Billy felt his hands ball into fists, and he stepped toward Kenwood.

Kenwood held his ground and looked toward the coach—who was staring their way. "Geez— what's his trouble?" Kenwood said, loud this time. "He had his three swings."

The coach jerked his head at Billy.

Billy had no choice but to keep moving. So he let it ride—this time.

Coach Anderson squinted at Kenwood. "Next pitcher," he called.

Jake the Fake took the mound. A left-hander like Billy, Jake had a windmilling, herky-jerky motion and today could not throw the ball through an open haymow door. After two batters and about twenty pitches, Coach Anderson came to the mound.

"Sorry, Coach," Jake said, tossing him the ball. "It's like I got webbed fingers or something."

"Too much you-know-what—" Tiny Tim said from the sidelines, and made a pumping motion with his right hand.

"Wrong hand," Jake said, walking off the mound, tugging at his crotch with his left hand.

"Crude gestures—take two laps, both of you," the coach said.

Tim groaned.

"You weenie—" Jake called after Tim, who sprinted away.

Jake galloped after him. "I'm gonna tack your weenie to a stump someday!" he shouted.

"Make it three laps," Coach Anderson said. He turned to Billy. "Next pitcher."

Trying to stay cool, Billy took the mound. He had pitched only once before, in the final game of last summer's season. Today the mound felt really high. Like he could fall off. Like he was exposed. He even forgot which foot went where.

"Start from the set position," the coach advised.

Billy nodded and positioned himself in front of the rubber, which felt solid against his left foot. A rubber was anchored, like a tree stump. Rolling the ball in his fingers, Billy took a deep breath, paused, then reared back and threw.

The ball soared high over the batter's head and rattled against the backstop.

There was laughter from the dugout, from Kenwood's group.

"Easy does it," Coach Anderson said.

"Just play catch with me," Butch added. He waggled his glove.

Billy swallowed and set himself again.

His second pitch was slower, and lower, but still chin high.

"Don't aim it, just throw," the coach added.

His third pitch was in there, and Billy felt himself relax. With each pitch after that he felt himself squeezing the ball less. He tried to let his legs and body do the work, to let the ball flow from his arm, his wrist, his hand, his fingers.

"Nice," the coach called. "Good control."

The batters stepped up one by one. Billy gradually expanded his motion. Soon he was pitching from a full windup. Hoist—kick—throw.

Hoist—kick—throw.

Hoist—kick—throw.

It felt good.

It felt better than good.

He wanted to make the feeling last. Last all spring. Last all summer, too. Because with Abner in jail Billy saw the writing on the wall—and it had little to do with baseball.

Hoist—kick—throw.

Hoist—kick—throw.

Then King Kenwood stood at the plate.

Billy blinked, set himself.

He tossed Kenwood two fat pitches. Kenwood smashed both of them through the infield. One just missed Billy's knee. The second whizzed past his ear.

"He's trying to hit the school's roof, like you did last summer," Tiny Tim called to Billy.

Billy squinted at Kenwood, then stepped off the rubber. He pretended to look carefully at the baseball in his hand. All the players in the dugout grew quiet. Billy stepped back on and readied himself for the third pitch. Kenwood crouched at the plate.

Billy gave him a lot of motion—but palmed the ball, which floated in at half speed. Kenwood was finished swinging before the ball cleared the mound—a clean whiff that sent him stumbling from the batter's box. There was silence in the dugout.

"Wait on him, just make contact," the coach called to King.

Kenwood flung away his bat.

At the end of practice, during cool-down laps, Kenwood trotted past Billy. "Sounds like you'll be needing some help on the farm this summer."

Billy jogged on without turning.

"Sloppin' the hogs, that sort of thing."

"Don't have any pigs. Not that you'd know the difference between cows and hogs."

"I'd come out and help, but I don't think I could stand the smell of shit."

Billy spun around but Kenwood dropped back, out of reach.

At the locker-room door Billy waited for the coach.

"Good practice, Billy!"

Billy nodded, but he was not smiling. "I hate to say this, Coach, but it was my last one."

"No way." The coach thought Billy was joking.

Billy nodded. "It's true. I'm through."

"You didn't let Kenwood get to you!" Coach Anderson began.

"Naw. Not that. It's my old man."

The coach's shoulders drooped. He set down his duffel bag.

"The farm and everything," Billy said.

The coach waited.

"I wanted to come today just to . . . show people," Billy murmured.

The coach smiled briefly. "It's been rough at school for you, I know," he said. "So coming today was the right move."

They were silent then. The coach frowned, bit his lip. He was thinking. "I suppose I could tell you to come to practice when you can," he said, "but it wouldn't be fair to the others. The ones who are here every day."

"I don't need any favors," Billy said sharply.

"Dammit," the coach muttered to himself. Finally he put on his best face and said, "Well, when school's out there's always City League summer baseball."

"Sure," Billy said. "Sure." He looked down briefly.

They shook hands, and Billy turned away.

The coach watched him go. Suddenly he called Billy's name.

Billy turned.

"Here—" the coach said. He reached into his duffel bag and tossed Billy a baseball, an orange baseball.

Billy caught the ball without taking his eyes from the coach.

"Keep it with you. I mean every day. Sleep with it. Count the stitches in the dark. Make it part of your hand."

Billy looked down at the bright baseball. He rolled it once in his palm. Then he nodded with a look that came almost to a smile, and turned away.

CHAPTER

8

On the farm Billy and his father planted oats. Twenty acres the first day. Nearly forty acres the next. Billy stayed home from school on Tuesday and Wednesday to help Abner finish the grain seeding. Mavis was not happy to do it, but wrote Billy a note excusing him from school. "It's a bad habit," she said with a stern look that included both Abner and Billy. "School ought to come first."

"Maybe it can for town kids," Abner said, "but not out here, in the country."

"It ought to come first for every kid," she countered.

Billy glanced around. He considered vamoosing, but luckily his parents did not argue for long; in the spring everyone was too busy for that. Mavis had her secretary's job at Doctors' Clinic plus the garden to get started. Billy and Abner had the grain and corn to plant. That day, and the whole next week, which was the first in May, they were too busy even to worry about Abner's troubles with the law. The three of them worked well into the evenings, which were warmer and longer now. It was finally spring in the high Midwest.

On Saturday Billy got stuck helping his mother in the garden. He had to plant peas. Four endless rows of peas. One inch deep, one inch apart, white seeds in the black dirt. Cover, tamp soil with boot. The rows seemed a mile long. Beside the garden was the big cornfield where Abner was planting with the tractor and seeder.

"He never plants corn before May fifteenth," Billy remarked to his mother. "What if it frosts?"

Mavis turned to stare across to the cornfield. "He wants to get it done in case . . ." Her words tapered off. She stared for long moments at the cornfield, then bent again to her own planting. "We'll just have to take our chances with the frost, won't we?"

From the garden Billy watched Abner's tractor move away down the field. It pulled the green planter with its four tall canisters full of yellow corn kernels; the tractor rumbled and the planter disks scraped. Billy bent back to his work. The endless rows of peas. In a while the tractor's noise grew louder again, and Billy stood upright to watch the turn. At field's end the skinny marker arm of the planter rose. Its smaller disk flashed once in the sunlight; then brakes groaned as the tractor swung sharply around, the opposite arm dropped and the tractor powered its way downfield again. If Abner stopped the tractor entirely, either at field's end or midfield, Billy could run to help him: Stopping meant either a mechanical breakdown or that it was time to refill the canisters with seed. Today, however, Abner's tractor kept moving.

As did Mavis. "Let's keep up on the peas," she called sharply to Billy. "Remember—we've got potatoes to plant."

Billy sighed louder and began to flick the hard and wrinkled peas into the trench as if he were shooting marbles. But he had fallen way behind his mother and now had to make up time; after a glance at her back, Billy took a huge handful of the peas and began to dribble them through his fingers as he walked quickly forward. As long as they hit somewhere, anywhere in the trench, he let the damn seeds lie where they fell.

"One inch apart, straight row," Mavis called to him without even looking.

Billy glared, muttered something that, luckily, Mavis did not hear, then trudged back to redo his work.

Sweet-corn planting was easier. At the end of the day, after the field corn was finished, Abner came around with the tractor and planter. The planter was empty. Billy measured a half coffee can of sweet-corn kernels into each canister. Then Abner carefully drove into the waiting garden; two quick passes with the tractor, and eight long rows of sweet corn were planted. That meant, later still, when the sweet corn was ankle high, Billy or Abner could drive between the rows with the tractor and attached cultivator. This eliminated most of the hoeing. Most. The whole garden was laid out that way, with rows forty inches apart, the same measurement as the field planter and cultivator. Anything to cut down on the damn hoeing.

Then, like a storm cloud swelling up dark and ugly on a sunny day, something came in the mail. It was a fat, gray, official-looking envelope from the Clerk of Court's office in town. Abner's court hearing was set for two weeks from Friday.

At supper nobody said much. Later that night Billy awoke to a creaking sound and a sharp, burning smell. He sniffed. Cigarette smoke. This was strange. Though Abner chewed tobacco, no one smoked on the Baggs farm.

Billy crept downstairs, followed the sound and the smell to the porch. There he saw his mother on the porch swing. She was smoking! Smoking and staring off into the darkness. Billy blinked his eyes and thought he might be having a weird dream. But sure enough, Mavis's cigarette glowed red above her fingers. The swing was moving in short jerks.

"How are we going to get along if you end up in jail?" she said.

At first Billy thought she was talking to herself.

Then, from the darker end of the porch, came the sound of his father shifting his boots. Slowly he came into focus, his sharp nose and chin in silhouette, pointing off across the dark fields.

"Billy can—" he began.

"He's only fourteen years old," Mavis said.

"That's old enough. It was for me."

"Well, he's not you. He's half me," she replied, "and I've got some say in this. Fourteen is still a boy, and I'm not going to let you work him like a full-grown man."

Abner's dark face turned to his wife, then back to the fields. The two of them were silent for a long while.

"I'm sorry," Mavis murmured. "I just get sick with worry."

"Well, don't," Abner said, and spit. "At least not yet. Who knows? Maybe we'll catch Judge Langen on a good day." Abner's brief laugh croaked across the yard.

Mavis was silent. Then her cigarette glowed deeply red—and quickly red again.

Billy retreated to his room. There he lay in bed with his eyes open in the dark. After a while he reached underneath his bed and found the orange baseball; still lying there, he began to turn its hard, round globe in his left hand. His fingers traced the stitches around and around—there were at least a hundred of them—until he finally fell asleep.

On Friday Abner dressed up in his black funeral suit. At least that was what Billy called it. Funerals were the only time he saw his father dressed up, and the last time had been for Robert's funeral.

"Why are you wearing that?" Mavis said immediately when she saw him. Her voice threatened to break. It was the black woolen suit that had come long ago from a brother who lived in California. Both of Abner's older brothers lived far away, in the West, and their wives occasionally sent boxes of out-of-style clothing back to Abner, who saw no problem in wearing perfectly good—and free—clothes. Trouble was, both his brothers were shorter and rounder men than Abner. Today, in the black suit, the white cuffs of Abner's shirt stuck out longer than chicken necks. The pants were too short also; Abner's boots, which Billy had shined himself, gleamed black and tall below the high cuffs. But no matter how out of character it looked, Billy could tell that the suit reminded her, too, of Robert's funeral.

"Why am I dressin' up? For my old buddy, Judge Langen," Abner said.

"That's not funny," Mavis replied. "Don't."

Abner shrugged and set his jaw.

When Mavis saw that Abner would not change his suit or his mind, she stepped forward to adjust his collar and tie. "I suppose this is all right," she murmured.

Abner grinned self-consciously. His black hair was slicked back with Vitalis.

Mavis stepped back to stare at him. "Wait," she said. She hustled back into the house and came back with her Kodak. "Lord knows this is no day for celebration, but how often do I see you dressed up?" She sighted through the camera.

Abner posed stiffly on the front steps. When his mouth was closed over his bad teeth, he was a handsome man, Billy thought. He could even be in movies. He would probably be the bad guy, but still Billy could see his father in the movies. Mavis fiddled with the camera. "Hurry it up," Abner called. "We can't be late for the hangin' judge."

Mavis lowered the camera. "Don't talk that way!" she said. Her voice was suddenly husky and more than a little angry; her eyes welled up with tears. Billy's own stomach felt funny. Then his mother raised the camera again and clicked the shutter.

At that instant Billy saw his father's smile fade. It was like he was thinking not of the camera but of Mavis. Like he was looking only at her. Like he was worrying about her. Abner's brown eyes were open, and one of his hands came partway up as if he wanted to say something. At that moment the camera clicked. The photograph turned out to be one of the best ever taken of Abner Baggs.

On the way to town, squeezed between his mother and father, and Abner's woolen suit smelling of camphor and mothballs, and the sunlight too bright in his eyes, Billy felt slightly dizzy. Everything was the same as that day when they had driven to town for Robert's funeral. Billy swallowed and looked past his mother to the window.

"Are you all right?"

Billy nodded. "I could use a little air," he murmured.

"Here, why don't we trade places," Mavis said.

Gratefully Billy took the passenger's side and rolled the window partway down. The air helped clear his head and settle his stomach, but things still felt too much like that day—

So he made himself think of Robert when he was alive, not lying in that—

Robert when the two of them were up to something good, or bad—it didn't matter as long as it was Robert alive—not lying there surrounded by flowers in that cold, hollow-sounding church—

Robert when he was—

Alive, with his quick, pure laugh that turned work into games, games into teasing, teasing into long laughing-and-crying big-brother little-brother afternoons when they were together all the time. Robert and the flash of his blue eyes and yellow hair. Robert with the sharp, square chin tipped with a pale sliver moon of a scar, where one day Billy had whacked him with a baseball bat.

Robert was teaching Billy to swing, standing close to Billy, lobbing him a rubber ball—then standing closer still, for Billy (five? six? years old at the time) was having no luck hitting the ball—no thanks to Robert's fake throws, and low throws, and high throws—anything but a strike.

"Harder!" Robert laughed, leaning closer still in this half-teasing game. "Swing harder!" And Billy, mad as a hornet, wound up and swung with all his might, spinning himself around not once but twice; and it was the second revolution that surprised them both. Pwop! The bat caught Robert square on the jaw and he was suddenly on his back, blinking up groggily at the high, blue sky, with blood streaming from his chin.

"How did this happen?" Abner growled as Mavis taped Robert's chin (he should have had stitches, but Abner decided those things). He glared at his two sons, who looked at each other in silence.

"That new calf kicked me," Robert said. "I was feeding it and it just reared back and let loose." He winked at Billy. . . .

And so Billy had left his mark on Robert that day.

Maybe that's what family is, Billy thought, *people who leave marks on each other.*

Billy forced himself back to the present, to the whine of the truck's tires on asphalt. He rode along for several miles in that zone of not thinking, the place of blankness that he had made for himself like some kids make a playhouse. It was a place to go to, a place to be while time passed until things got better. He was vaguely aware of the murmur of his parents' voices, of his mother asking what to do about this, about that, if . . .

"Well, we'll soon enough find out, won't we?" Abner said as he slowed for the Flint city-limits sign.

Mavis dabbed at her eyes with a handkerchief,

then straightened in the seat.

The courthouse parking lot was nearly full. Knots of people lingered on the courthouse steps. "Wonder what's going on today," Abner said.

"You are," Mavis said.

"Me?" Abner said. A narrow grin came onto his lips.

As the Baggs family headed up the courthouse steps, several men, some farmers but some from town as well, stepped forward to shake Abner's hand. "Good luck, Baggs!"

"He had it comin'."

"He was a crook, that Meyers."

Abner nodded, shook hands here and there. For a moment he seemed like a popular politician, but Mavis did not look around her as they climbed the sharp granite steps. The big courthouse doors loomed ahead of them; Billy's guts tied themselves in a single, hard knot. He could barely breathe.

"Jailbird Baggs," someone whispered.

Billy whirled around. In the crowd, waiting outside the courthouse, were King Kenwood and a couple of his friends. He lunged toward them, but Mavis caught his sleeve and yanked him back. "No," she whispered sharply. "Don't make things worse."

At the back of the crowd he saw a flash of silvery-blonde ponytail—Suzy Langen. Her face was bunched to a frown. For a frozen moment

Billy and Suzy stared at each other. "I'm sorry . . ." she mouthed.

Then Billy was swept along. Coach Anderson appeared from nowhere and shook hands with Abner and the whole family. "This way, please," someone said, and they passed through tall doors that closed behind them and led to a smaller hearing room.

Suddenly it was silent. The bailiff motioned for them to be seated. Judge Langen's big, empty desk loomed before them. They sat and waited several minutes. A clock ticked. Then the county attorney, Mark Kenwood, entered, followed by Doyle James, a pale and pudgy lawyer, the cheapest one in town.

"I don't see how you can say that," James was protesting.

"I can say it because that's the law," Kenwood said sharply. "Take it or leave it."

Mavis glanced worriedly to Billy. Then the rear door opened and Judge Langen himself strode in. He was a commanding figure in his black robes, his full head of sandy-colored hair turning to silver at the sides, his square jaw. He looked at no one.

"All rise," someone said.

"I just got sat down," Abner muttered, loud enough for everyone to hear; Mavis jabbed him in the ribs with her elbow. Slowly, grudgingly, making a big production of it, Abner stood up. Judge Langen arched one eyebrow as he glanced toward Abner Baggs. Then he settled in at his desk, shrugged on his reading glasses and began to page through sheets of paper.

Everyone sat down, and quickly enough, in language that Billy did not understand, the judge and the attorneys spoke back and forth. Abner's attorney had a soft voice and seemed uncertain about nearly everything. He kept saying, "No contest, your honor. . . . We don't deny that, your honor. . . ."

And Judge Langen, after scribbling some notes, said, without looking up, "I hereby impose upon Abner Baggs restitution in the amount of six thousand dollars—"

There was a sucking-in of breath from Mavis.

"—and sentence him, commencing today, to not less than sixty days in the county jail, with three hundred and five days suspended on condition of good behavior and full payment of the six thousand dollars."

Abner Baggs laughed. It was a harsh, defiant laugh that echoed in the chambers.

"Correction. Make that ninety days," Judge Langen said.

"Please—Judge, don't!" Mavis called out as she jumped to her feet. "He—he didn't mean anything. He didn't mean to laugh."

Langen took off his glasses. "I have an idea. Why don't we ask Mr. Baggs himself."

All eyes turned to Abner, who slowly stood up. "Six years ago there was a bad accident in our family. My oldest boy, Robert, was killed in a tractor accident. "

Billy looked suddenly down; he gripped his chair and held on to it to keep the room from spinning—to hold off that jerking, out-of-control feeling—the same feeling on the tractor that day . . .

"It was an election year and you made a big deal of it with your investigation, your call for more laws about safety on the farm."

"I fail to see the relevancy—"

"Relevancy? I'll tell you the relevancy," Abner said. "You got yourself elected from county attorney to judge—all because of my family's tragedy."

"This makes no sense," the judge began.

"Then you stick up for crooks like Randy Meyers," Abner continued, his voice rising to a hoarse shout, "because you don't give a damn about anyone who lives an inch beyond the city limits of this town."

Judge Langen's gavel fell like the report of a small-caliber rifle. "Ninety days, commencing now. And get him out of here before I make it six months." A police officer led the cursing Abner out a side door, the judge's black robes disappeared through the back door and Billy and his mother were ushered out the front.

Just outside the hearing room, Coach Anderson quickly stepped forward to walk with Billy and Mavis. In a halting voice she told him the sentence, and the news raced down the crowded hallway like lightning along a wire fence. Among the faces King Kenwood's came into focus. He was looking at Billy and grinning. "Told you so," he whispered.

In an instant Billy was on him, flailing away, punching, crying, hitting at Kenwood, at anyone or anything that moved.

CHAPTER 9

At home, where warm May sunlight shone on the farm, Mavis and Billy stayed inside the house. They sat in the kitchen. The coach was there, too. Billy had a scrape on his cheek, and his left knuckles were split open and bandaged. He also had a date with the social worker. Abner was in jail.

"Least they could have let Abner come home, get some of his things," Mavis said. Her eyes were red.

The coach nodded in agreement. He looked at the calendar on the wall, briefly out the window, then to Mavis. "So how are you going to manage? I mean the farm."

Mavis glanced at Billy, then back to the coach.

"We can do it," Billy said. He set his jaw.

"No, we can't," Mavis said, "not all of it."

"Yes, we can," Billy said immediately.

Mavis shook her head sideways. "Most, maybe, but not all. Abner and I have to talk. We're going to need some local help. Maybe Dale Schwartz can do some of the tractor work."

"Not Schwartz," Billy said sharply.

"Why not? Beggars can't be choosers right now," Mavis said, anger in her voice.

The coach blinked. His eyes went to the calendar, then quickly back to Mavis. He was thinking. Thinking. He cleared his throat. "This might well be the wrong time to bring this up," he began, "but I had hopes that Billy could play City League summer baseball."

There was louder silence in the kitchen. Billy looked at Mavis. Her eyes began to brim with tears. Before she could open her mouth, Billy himself spoke. "I don't have no time for summer baseball," he said. "I got a farm to run."

At school, now at the very end of the year, things were no better. The coach was meeting with the principal to discuss the "Billy problem." Billy, not reacting kindly to whispers in the hallway of "Jailbird Baggs," had sent two boys, on two successive days, to the school nurse. One boy had a bloody nose, the other a chipped front tooth. Right now Billy himself sat at lunch in the cafeteria, toying with his Spanish rice and fruit cup, pretending he was not worried about the outcome of the coach's meeting.

"Here he comes!" whispered Tiny Tim.

"So?" Billy said.

"Billy," the coach said, waving Billy his way, "can we talk a minute?"

"Here is fine," Billy answered, setting his jaw. He sat at one of the back tables, where the country kids and Indian students congregated; Butch Redbird sat on one side, Tiny Tim Loren on the other.

"Suit yourself," the coach said.

"So what's the verdict?" Billy said, attempting

a laugh, which came out too high-pitched, squeaky like his father's.

"Good news, bad news," the coach said.

Billy waited.

"Suspension—but only one day."

"Why not make it a full-time suspension?" Billy said sarcastically.

"What do you mean by that?" Coach said.

"He means if he was sixteen, he'd quit school," Tiny Tim piped up.

Billy stared defiantly at Coach Anderson.

"Quit school?" The coach paused; he looked down at Billy's plate. "You can't quit school. Where you gonna find Spanish rice like that except here at school?"

Billy's eyes traveled slowly down to his plate. To the sticky globs of red rice.

Butch Redbird and Tiny Tim grinned. Then, slowly, so did Billy. As the coach walked away, they began to laugh like crazy, and soon enough to push Spanish rice into each other's faces.

Billy's suspension passed, and so, quickly, did the remaining days of school. The excitement of the last two weeks of school took the focus off Billy. There were no more fights—but that was because Coach Anderson had volunteered for extra hall duty and so kept his eyes on Billy.

The last day of school, however, was touch and go.

At noon hour there were loud hoots and whistling from the front steps. Billy, in the group of outsiders that hung off to the side, looked around.

Across the street, raking the City Park, was the work crew from the jail. They were dressed in orange coveralls and one of them limped as he worked.

"It's old man Baggs," Nix Nixon shouted with glee. Kenwood himself stood on the steps, pretending to examine his fingernails.

"The Crrrazy Car Crusher!" Nixon called.

Some of the jail crew stopped raking and looked up, first at the school steps, then at Abner.

Abner kept raking. The sweeps of his arms were long and powerful, pulling him steadily away ahead of the others. He was a raking machine.

"Hey—Sheet-Metal Baggs!" Nixon persisted.

Keeping his rake moving with one arm, and without looking at the crowded school steps, Abner Baggs raised his other arm and hand and extended a long middle finger to the entire school.

The students whooped with delight.

Billy angled through the crowd, his cheeks scarlet with rage. He scattered people as he arrowed toward Nixon and Kenwood. "Billy, don't—" Suzy Langen called, but even her voice had no effect. The Kenwood circle tightened around its leader and got ready for Billy—but the coach leaped into the middle of things. "Easy does it, Billy." He hooked his shoulder and neck in a half nelson; Billy strained forward but the coach had him. "Easy!"

"I'll kill them!" Billy said. His eyes burned with a hard blue light.

"Nixon, see me inside," the coach barked.

Nixon looked quickly at his group, to Kenwood—all of whom pretended to be talking to someone else. Nixon's face darkened and he resignedly headed up the steps and through the door.

To Billy the coach said, "Get through today and school's out, Billy." He spoke softly, so no one else could hear. "Next school year everything will be different. Everybody will have forgotten."

Billy glared at Kenwood, at the other town kids. "Except me," he breathed.

A t the jail, country music twanged from a cheap radio. Billy was there, along with Coach Anderson; it was the coach who had talked Billy into visiting Abner in his cell.

"Baggs? Sure. Go on back," the night deputy said to the coach. He was eating some fried chicken that looked homemade and good. He wiped his fingers and stood up to unlock the main door. The lock turned and clicked again behind the coach.

They passed along the ten or so cells, all of which were full. There was a faint smell of urine and old clothes, and the sound of snoring.

Abner sat up and stared through the open door of his cell. "Well, well. Step in. Pull up a couple of chairs."

There weren't any chairs.

The coach smiled; it was Abner's kind of joke.

"Evening," he said to Abner. "Billy and I were in the neighborhood."

"Well, ain't that nice, you and Billy," Abner

said, raising one eyebrow at the coach. But fortunately he let the matter drop. Across, stretched out on the opposite bunk, reading the local newspaper, was a large Indian man with a long, thick, black braid.

"Not a lot of room in the Flint County Ritz," Abner added, "but we get by here, don't we, Chief?"

The Indian man moved only his eyeballs as he cast a baleful sideways look at Abner.

"Pleased to meet you," the coach said pleasantly to Abner's cell mate, and stepped forward to shake hands. "Oswald Anderson."

The Indian man, George Wind, slowly raised his middle finger at them as he continued to read his newspaper.

"He don't say much more than that," Abner said. "So him and me get along just fine."

The coach looked around, cast about for a new topic. On the floor was a picnic basket with the remains of chicken bones, potatoes and gravy— home cooking. "What's this? Room service?"

"Mavis thinks I'll get skinny on jail food."

"Get?" George Wind murmured.

"What's that?" Abner said sharply.

Wind kept reading.

"That chief will drive me crazy, I swear," Abner muttered. They were silent for a spell.

"So. Anything you need?" the coach ventured. "Anything I can help out with?"

Abner croaked his brief, sarcastic laugh. "What

more could a man want than this?" He gestured to his cell.

"How about the farm?"

"What about it?"

"All the work."

"Billy's there. He can handle it."

"It's a lot for—"

"He can handle it," Abner repeated, "right, Billy?"

"Sure, Pa."

The coach let the subject drop. He looked around the bare cell. There was only a deck of cards. "You need any books? Magazines?"

"Naw. I ain't much of a reader," Abner said quickly. He looked across the cell. "Not like some people."

George Wind kept reading.

They were silent again.

"I play an occasional hand of poker, though," Abner added.

"Poker?" the coach said casually. "I've been known to play the game." In truth he and a group of teachers played a good deal of poker during the long winter.

Abner reached for the deck of cards and began to shuffle them.

The coach cut the cards and Abner dealt. His long fingers were quick and sure with the cards. George Wind lowered his magazine and leaned in to watch.

An hour later the coach was out $4.80 and

very late for dinner. "Fold," the coach said.

Abner hooted a single laugh as the coach forked over five dollars.

"Here's your change," Abner said, handing back two dimes. "These used to belong to the chief," he said. He laughed again.

George Wind gave Abner and the coach another middle finger, then returned to his reading.

Abner followed the coach and Billy to the door and waited there while the night deputy unlocked the heavy lock. "How you getting home?" Abner asked Billy.

"Coach will drop me off."

Abner was silent a moment. Billy waited for a typical Abner remark, such as "We ain't in the habit of depending on someone for rides" or "Next time you walk."

But his father swallowed and said, gruffly, "I appreciate that, Coach."

Billy's eyes widened.

"You're welcome—" the coach said, as surprised as Billy.

"But let's not make a habit of it," Abner directed Billy.

"Sure, Pa," Billy said, holding back a smile.

"Although he's welcome to come back anytime and play poker," Abner added. He meant to say it sarcastically, but it came out more like an actual invitation. Like Abner could use the company.

The two men looked at each other.

"I will," the coach said. "And I'm damn well bringing my own deck of cards."

Abner grunted part of a laugh, then turned back with his limping stride to his bunk.

Back on the farm, on the first morning of summer vacation, Billy sat on the porch steps with his baseball glove. He gave it a few slaps, then abruptly got up and stashed the glove back in the closet. Hung it up for good. Summer "vacation," what a laugh—a double laugh this year. Summer was never any kind of vacation on the farm, and this summer, with his father in jail, Billy could see ahead of him only double the work.

Corn cultivating.

Haying.

Oat harvesting.

The garden.

And always the dairy cows. They had to be milked twice a day, every day.

Skinner came loping up to Billy. "What do you want?" Billy said gruffly. The old black Labrador with the gray muzzle carried his well-chewed rubber baseball and wagged his tail hopefully. "As if I didn't know," Billy muttered. From habit he tugged on the ball; from habit Skinner held on—

then let go. Billy rolled the slimy old ball in his fingers.

"Okay, okay, one toss," Billy said, "but I've got work to do." He was supposed to hoe the garden, clean the gutter and first calf pen, then visit Abner in jail that afternoon for some instructions. Work instructions, no doubt.

"Sit!"

Skinner crouched at Billy's side.

"Stay!"

Skinner moaned and twitched under the torment of waiting.

Billy flung the ball high into the air. "Fetch!"

Skinner sprang forward like a deer from its bed. He raced forward, tracking the ball's descent—then leaped and caught it several feet off the ground. "Good boy!" Billy called. "For a geezer dog you sure can jump."

He gave the ball a few more throws, and Skinner caught it in the air each time. Soon enough, however, Skinner's pink tongue and his vertical jump were both dragging the dirt, and it was time for Billy to get serious about work. He pocketed the ball, and Skinner slumped off to find shade. With Skinner gone the whole yard stood silent—as if it was waiting for Billy to get busy.

He scanned the farmstead. In the garage was Abner's pickup. Mavis had gotten a ride to her job in town with Mrs. Pederson. The pickup had to remain home, they agreed; Billy might need it for errands, for emergencies. It was agreed that Billy could drive the pickup for parts, for pulling the wagon of cow feed to the Feedmill in town, plus whatever other farming reasons arose. Billy had no driver's license—not even his driving permit—but in Flint County (there were understood rules about this issue) the sheriff and the city police always cut farm kids some slack. As long as the kids looked sixteen, as long as they drove mainly on the back roads, and as long as they appeared to be on farm business, there was no problem. Mavis was not happy about the idea of Billy driving to town by himself, but sometimes he might have to see Abner for advice on this or that, so what could she do?

Billy checked the sun. Hell, there was still plenty of morning left. He hopped into the pickup. Skinner, upon hearing the truck door slam, mustered energy for one more jump—into the back. "I've got an emergency need for an orange pop," Billy said to him, and backed the truck sharply about. "What say we head down to Bob's Barn?"

Skinner barked twice.

"Plus we might stop by the Erickson place and check on Gina and Heather. It's the neighborly thing to do, right?"

Skinner barked again, and Billy dropped his foot off the clutch pedal. The tires spun gravel, and seconds later they were jolting down the long driveway at high speed.

Billy roared along the graveled back roads with one arm out the window, his hand planing the soft June air, the other hand loosely on the wheel. He wished the truck had a radio. Suddenly—around a sharp corner—there was the road grader, a tall iron giraffe of a machine plodding along at ten miles an hour. Billy grabbed the wheel with both hands and braked hard—but no way could he slow enough. Trusting his luck, Billy swung around the grader—just in time to see another pickup dead ahead. He recognized the truck: a blue, battered Ford driven by Herman Hoistad, a crabby old bachelor farmer.

Hoistad leaned on his horn and steered far to the right. Billy arrowed in front of the grader, skidded back to his side of the road in a cloud of dust—and gave old Herman the middle finger. The geezer shook his fist at Billy, who laughed and sped along even faster. Skinner barked his approval, and his ears streamed straight back in the wind.

At the Erickson place, a trailer house and some low sheds tucked into the pines, Billy rattled up the driveway and braked to halt. A cloud of dust rolled forward past the truck.

Gina Erickson, age twelve going on twenty-one, appeared at the trailer door. She had on smudged terry-cloth shorts, a dirtier T-shirt and clearly no bra. On both Erickson girls it was their chests that grew faster than any other parts of their bodies; both sisters were stubby in the legs but big on top. Last year Gina's T-shirts had covered two nubbins as small as a little calf's horns, but this year they were as big as baseballs. "Well, if it ain't Billy Baggs," Gina said, posing against the trailer door.

Heather appeared behind her sister. Both girls had wild, reddish hair. Their mother worked at the nursing home in town, two shifts; their father was long gone. Billy didn't remember him.

"Your old man still in jail?" Gina said.

Billy shrugged. "Yeah."

"You visit him yet?"

"Supposed to this afternoon."

"He know you're out driving around?"

"So what if he does?" Billy said.

Gina smiled at that.

"Where you going?"

"Bob's."

"Wait up—" both girls said at once.

Once the three of them were inside the cab, Billy glanced down at Heather's tie-dyed rainbow T-shirt. Two wet spots had appeared on the front; just from walking to the truck she was leaking milk.

"How's the kid?" Billy said, putting the truck in reverse. He supposed the baby must be with Heather's mother, or with somebody.

Heather looked at him; her eyes widened. "Stop the truck!"

Billy braked hard.

"For God's sakes!" Gina said, as Heather swung open the door. "How can you forget your own baby?"

"Go to hell—you didn't remember him either!" Heather called back.

"He ain't my kid."

Billy and Gina watched her head for the trailer. "She does that all the time," Gina said to Billy, "forgets she has him. How can you forget you have a kid?"

"Maybe if he had a name?" Billy ventured.

Heather, hearing that, gave them both the middle finger, then disappeared inside to get the baby. Within seconds she returned carrying a blanketed bundle. "I'll give him a damn name when I feel like giving him a damn name and not before," Heather said. She climbed back into the truck.

"Sure, fine—" Billy said quickly. He glanced down at the little, dark-haired boy. He was sleeping soundly, a smile on his face.

"I just ain't thought of the right one yet," Heather said, holding him tightly to her chest.

On the way back from Bob's, where Billy spent three whole dollars on pop, candy and a pack of cigarettes, Gina said, "Let's go swimming. At Riverbend."

"Got to get back," Billy said. "I'm runnin' the farm this summer." Smoke from his cigarette swirled back through the window and up his nose. He coughed.

"It's too cold anyway," Heather said.

"It ain't cold. You just don't want to go swimming 'cause you're too fat," Gina said.

"Shut up!" Heather said.

"Big as a cow!"

"Knock it off, you two," Billy said.

"She thinks she's ugly now," Gina said, turning to Billy. "She told me so. Now that she's got a kid, men don't look at her like they used to."

"She's full of shit," Heather said, ignoring Gina by looking out the window.

"They look at me instead."

"So full of it her eyeballs are turning brown."

"It's true," Gina said. Sitting in the middle, she leaned closer to Billy and rested one round, firm breast against his shoulder. "Ain't it, Billy?"

Billy looked across to Heather. "Heather's not ugly," Billy said. "A little bigger, maybe, but not ugly, no way."

Heather managed part of a smile. Then Billy saw her eyes glisten. She was close to crying.

"Hell, I'd swim with her any day," Billy said.

At Riverbend, the local swimming hole, which was hidden from the road by thick brush and trees, there were no other cars or people.

"All to ourselves—I told you so!" Gina said.

Skinner was the first one out. Before Billy had stopped the truck, Skinner soared over the side and disappeared through the brush. As Billy and the girls exited the truck, they heard a tremendous splash.

"Come on," Gina said, skipping forward. "What are you afraid of?"

"Nothin'," Heather said sullenly.

When Billy and Heather arrived at the river's edge and the big boulder, Gina's clothes lay in a pile on the rock. "God, it's cold!" Gina shrieked as she surfaced in the middle of the stream.

Heather stood there, holding the baby, looking down at the river. The water was high; it was always high in early summer. High and dark and cold. A branch came snaking by, twisting, spinning in the current. She stepped closer to the water's edge.

"Come on! Chickens!" Gina shouted. She swam closer and hoisted herself partway up on one of the river rocks.

Billy looked at Heather, then back to Gina.

Gina hunched there, water shining on her shoulders and the tops of her round, brand-new breasts. She grinned at Billy. She did not mind how much he saw.

Heather just kept holding her baby and staring down at the swift-moving water. She took another step closer.

"Hey, hurry up," Billy said to Gina, keeping one eye on her and one on Heather. "We ain't got all day."

"Ain't you comin' in?"

"Not today," Billy said. Gina spit water and splashed away, but Billy stayed close to Heather and the baby.

On the way back to the Erickson house it was only Gina who shivered and smelled like river water. Though the day was plenty warm and the river inviting, Billy had not wanted to leave Heather too much alone. Last summer they had all splashed around in their birthday suits. This summer things were more serious; this summer there were four of them. Billy didn't like the way Heather stood there on the rocks, holding the baby; something about her and the baby and the water gave him the willies.

Then again, he didn't imagine it was easy, having a kid at age sixteen, especially when the father was Dale Schwartz, the local loser who had gotten Heather drunk one night last August. Schwartz was nearly thirty years old, and would be charged with rape if Heather ever went to the sheriff. So far she hadn't.

"Have you thought any more about a name for the baby?" Billy ventured.

"No," Heather said briefly.

"You got to do it sooner or later," Gina said.

"Says who?" Heather retorted.

Billy and Gina glanced at each other.

"I think there's some kind of law," Gina said.

"There ain't any law. I checked on it," Heather said.

They drove along in silence.

"Mama wants to call him Victor," Gina ventured, "after Victor in *The Young and the Restless*."

"She can't call him Victor or any other name,"

Heather said flatly. "It's my baby, not hers."

"So why don't you name it?"

"I told you. I ain't thought of the right one yet."

"Some mother you are," Gina said, and spit out the window.

"Shut up!" This time it was Billy who said it to Gina.

"You wait," Heather said to her sister. "Someday it'll be your turn."

"Not me," Gina said immediately. "I ain't gettin' myself knocked up."

"Right," Heather said sarcastically. "It'll be your turn real soon if you go around showing off your tits like you do for Billy."

"I don't mind," Billy replied slyly.

Gina giggled.

"Not that they're worth looking at." Heather sniffed.

"Least they're not big old jugs of milk like yours!"

"They will be soon, you keep fooling around."

"Shut up."

"You shut up."

"You shut up!"

The Erickson sisters were still squabbling as Billy let them off at their trailer. In his rearview mirror he saw Heather set the baby down on the ground and pick up a corncob and fling it at Gina—who gave her sister the finger and skipped just out of range. Heather chased her briefly. The baby lay alone in his blanket on the ground. Billy stopped the pickup until he saw Heather return and retrieve the baby. He stared. "I know what they ought to name that boy," Billy said to Skinner. "Lucky. They ought to call him Lucky. He's sure gonna need some."

Skinner barked in agreement, and Billy drove on. Some distance down the road, he squinted up at the sun; he realized it was nearly noon and he hadn't done a lick of work. The road was damp and knife-blade smooth from the grader's passage, and Billy brought the old Ford's speed up to sixty. As he drove, he thought of Suzy Langen: He imagined her swimming in the deep, blue water of Riverbend. He pictured her pale hair drifting free in the slow current, pictured her long, tanned legs slowly kicking, holding her in place. She was perfect. If only she had a different last name.

Taking back roads, Billy drove to town. He entered Flint from the north, a route that brought him past Green Lawn, Flint's only suburb, a development of curving streets with modern rambler homes and trimmed shrubbery and tidy curbs. It was where Suzy Langen lived.

At 1869 Venus Lane, to be exact (Billy had looked up the address in the phone book), and now he turned onto her actual street. His heart flip-flopped like a rooster in a gunnysack. He took a deep breath. A couple of women walking for exercise, wearing white shorts and sun visors, turned their heads to stare at him as he passed.

Make that glare at him.

Or at least Billy imagined that they did.

Which brought out the Abner in him, brought out the anger. So what if he was wearing a dusty cap and driving a rusted farm pickup? Where was the law against driving down Venus Lane? Billy gave the two women a quick look at his middle finger. In his rearview mirror he saw them straighten their spines as if a couple of bumblebees had stung them in the ass.

Ahead a block and on the right was Suzy's house. He slowed, though not so much as to be obvious, and stared at the trimmed lawn and perfectly clipped shrubbery. The landscaping flowed to a sidewalk that curved up to the one-story brick house. In front, facing the street, was a large, low picture window. Billy could see right inside the living room. There was a big TV, a sunburst clock on the wall, lots of pale couches and chairs, a china cabinet. The Langen house and yard looked cleaner, even, than the coach's place. He wondered if Suzy mowed the lawn. If she trimmed the shrubs. If she had to do any kind of work.

In the Langen backyard there was a swimming pool, the above-ground kind, about four feet high. Several heads bobbed, and water lapped over the side. Suddenly a girl cannonballed into view; water sprayed upward and rainbowed in the sunlight. He braked almost to a stop. He watched the girls splash in the pool. He could hear the sounds of the water, their laughing voices.

"Excuse me!" someone said.

Billy's eyes widened.

The two women who had been walking were coming up fast in his mirror.

"You there!"

Billy hit the gas pedal and accelerated away with a squeal of tires. From the corner of his eye he saw Suzy herself stand up in the pool and look toward the street. Water gleamed down the planes of her body, and she shaded her eyes to look toward him.

Damn!

And worse, Billy watched one of the women in white shorts glare at the truck for real this time—likely taking his license plate—then turn up the sidewalk to the Langen house. It was Suzy's mother.

"Double damn!" Driving faster still, the tires chirping, he exited the curved streets of Green Lawn and headed downtown. If she was thinking about calling the police, at least Billy would be at the one spot they would never look: the county jail.

But Abner was not at "home."

"He's on a raking crew," the jailor said from his chair in the front office. He rolled a toothpick in his mouth as he gave Billy a long once-over stare. "City Park's where you'll find him."

Billy vamoosed. He was glad Abner was gone. He didn't like the jail. The lobby and visiting area were okay, but in the back, where the cells were, where Abner stayed, was creepy.

Keeping his eyes peeled for cops, Billy drove down to the Flint City Park, a narrow strip of grass and trees and picnic tables that lay between the main highway and the river. It was a popular rest stop for passing tourists; several motor homes and station wagons were parked there, engine lids propped open, motors cooling, as families sat at wooden tables eating or else walking their little dogs.

Tourists and jailbirds.

To the left side, working their way toward the middle of the park and the picnic tables, were Abner and the raking crew. They all wore orange coveralls. The tourist parents kept their eyes on the men as they worked.

Abner was well ahead of the other rakers. His long arms pulled him forward. The rest of the gang was a mix of Indian and white men, including George Wind, whose brown chest and arms swelled out of his coveralls like bread bulging out of its baking tin; his coveralls were at least three sizes too small.

As Billy drove up, Abner paused to lean on his rake and stare.

Billy was careful to drive slowly, to stop smoothly.

"'Bout time," Abner said as Billy hopped out.

"Chores," Billy explained.

"Got the gutter cleaned?"

"Sure," Billy lied. He could not believe how fast the day was moving. In a couple of hours he would have to feed grain and get ready for the evening milking.

"That steer okay? The one with the lame leg?"

"He's getting around," Billy said, which was true.

"And old Stretchy? She milking any better?"

"A lot better," Billy said quickly, then glanced off to the river.

"Don't be overgraining those cows. The grass is plenty good enough right now."

Billy nodded.

The rest of the work crew had caught up with Abner now. "You on vacation, hey?" George said to Abner.

"I already raked twice as much you, Chief," Abner said without a glance.

George winked at Billy. "Your old man, he's a raking fool."

"That's why the sheriff put me in charge," Abner said. "I'm the only one knows how to work around here."

"Slave driver," George said. The other men nodded their agreement.

"You see, the white man is naturally the harder worker," Abner explained to Billy. "That's why we ended up in charge of this country."

"But I say why work yourself to the bone?" George said. "You know what that gets you?"

"What?" Abner said, and spit exasperatedly to one side.

"Skinny," George said.

There were snickers of laughter from the crew. Even Billy had to bite back a grin.

Abner glared at his gang. "Keep movin'! This ain't some kind of union shop."

With exaggerated slowness, the rakes began to sweep once again. "Slow and steady wins the race, I say," George said.

"Insubordinate today, too," Abner said. "Maybe I'll have to chat with the sheriff about you, Chief."

"Don't matter if you do or if you don't. White men all gonna have heart attacks, anyway. Fifty years from now the Indians will be back on top."

The Indians chuckled and kept raking.

Very slowly.

"So as I was saying," Abner said to Billy, ignoring the crew, "we got one little business item to take care of." He lowered his voice, pulled Billy to one side and began to speak to him.

Billy listened.

"The key is in the milk house." Abner was speaking of his lockbox that he kept in the attic. Billy had never seen it open. "It's hung up on the top shelf."

"Okay," Billy said.

"But the lockbox itself ain't in the attic no more," Abner said. "I moved it in case somebody tries to break in now that I'm gone."

"They're not gonna break in," Billy said.

"Easy to do when nobody's home," Abner said, raising one eyebrow to Billy.

Billy kept his gaze steady.

"Anyway, the lockbox is in the granary, up in the rafters, under some feed sacks. It's got enough money in it to pay Meyers and then some."

"Six thousand dollars?" Billy said.

"Keep your voice down, dammit!" Abner hissed, glancing around at the jail crew. "This ain't no church choir."

"I thought you weren't going to pay it," Billy whispered.

Abner paused. There was silence. He looked down at his hands, at the rake, then up at Billy. "If I don't, Langen will keep me in here for a year."

Billy swallowed. He looked off toward the river.

"Bein' in jail ain't any fun," Abner said softly. "Sometimes at night with all the guys snoring and farting and groaning and whimpering in their sleep, and the police radio squawking all hours of the night, and the cars outside racing and honking—well, I think I might go crazy." There was something in his voice that made Billy keep staring off at the river; it was something weak, something nearly beaten.

"So we'll pay Meyers the damn restitution—but with a little twist," Abner said, recovering the hard edge to his voice; he might be down, but he wasn't out for the count, not Abner Baggs. He pulled Billy closer, whispered his plan.

Billy drew back. "We're gonna get in more trouble."

"How so?" Abner said. "Judge Langen says I have to pay the fine. Did he say how I should pay it?"

"No," Billy had to admit.

"That's right. Money is money. Here's how we're gonna do it." He spoke low and further to Billy.

"Okay," Billy murmured, "but still—"

"But nothing. Judge Langen says pay, I'll pay." He hooted a brief laugh, and a sharp, gleaming light burned in his eyes.

The rake crew stood staring at them.

"What? Who are you guys waiting for, Custer? Get those rakes going!" Abner barked.

The men set slowly to work. Billy headed toward the truck.

"One more thing," Abner called out to Billy.

Billy turned to look back.

"I know exactly how much money is in there."

Billy set his jaw and turned away. In the truck, as he started the engine, he saw Abner begin raking again—raking toward the nearest picnic table full of tourists. Raising dust and grass and pine needles with each sweep, Abner homed in on them.

The parents of a tidy family of four, with a small terrier and two kids and a bright-red Coleman cooler, watched him draw near. Abner didn't look up. Soon pinecones were bouncing around their feet.

"Excuse me—sir—could you—" The father stood and pointed off to the side, away from his family. He spoke pleasantly enough.

Abner kept raking straight toward the tourists. Dust rolled toward them and their food. The rest of the raking crew stopped to watch. They began to grin.

The tourists' dog began to yap wildly and lunge at Abner.

The mother looked uncertainly at her children. Suddenly she whispered something to them, and they scrambled into the motor home.

"Would it be possible for you to rake over there?" the man said to Abner. "As you can see, we're trying to have our lunch here."

Abner kept raking straight toward them.

The father glanced toward the motor home. His wife grabbed up their cooler and the dog, and within seconds the parents, too, clambered inside. The door locked sharply behind them, and in another few seconds the big tin schooner lurched onto the highway. Behind, on the table, sat their picnic lunch. Abner glanced after the motor home, then inspected the food. He picked up the sandwich with the least bites gone and began to chew on it. "Take a break, boys," he called, waving his crew forward. "Lunch is served."

Back home, in the attic of the granary, Billy sneezed as he moved dusty feed sacks. Sure enough, there was the lockbox. It was welded steel, homemade of course, and the size of a medium suitcase.

The key turned smoothly in the padlock, and Billy opened the hasp.

He sucked in his breath at the sight of the

money. The box was nearly half full! Green stacks of twenty-dollar bills, dozens, *hundreds* of twenties, were tied with string and piled in even rows. Each stack had a little note atop:

Saved June–August 1955
Saved January–April 1961

And so on, back for years.

Twenty-dollar bills saved from the milk check.

Twenty-dollar bills saved from cattle sold to market.

Twenty-dollar bills saved from corn and lumber sold.

Each stack was tied with string.

Each stack contained five hundred dollars.

Billy counted the stacks, then breathed out a long breath. There were close to twenty thousand dollars here.

He leaned away to think. He looked down at the dusty, mouse-chewed boards of the granary. At the worn scoop shovel in the corner.

With twenty thousand dollars they could buy a better tractor.

And an electric grain auger.

And a silo unloader.

And a manure conveyor.

And a pipeline milking system.

They could add onto the house.

They could—

But he stopped himself. It was Abner's money,

not his, and he wondered, momentarily, if Mavis knew how much cash was here. After he counted out the six thousand dollars, he looked one more time at the stash of green bills in the trunk. "I'll have my own money someday," Billy muttered. "Two trunks, clear full of it."

On Saturday Billy drove a wagonful of corn and oats to town. Mavis rode along in the truck. "I still don't like you driving without your license," she said.

Billy glanced over at her.

"Though you're a good enough driver, I suppose," she added.

"I am?" Billy said, looking her way for long moments, pretending that he had forgotten to watch the road.

"Stop that," she said, laughing.

Billy slowed carefully at the city-limits sign, passing what used to be Randy Meyers A-1 Cars. The flattened, burned hulks of cars still sat there, along with the crushed building. It was rumored that as soon as Meyers got his six-thousand-dollar restitution payment from Abner, he was going to rebuild, to get back in business.

"I wish we'd never stopped there that time," Mavis murmured. "I should have known better."

"You did the right thing," Billy said.

Mavis looked over at him.

"It's just Pa," Billy added. "He's . . ."

They looked at each other.

"He's who he is," Mavis finished.

"Yeah," Billy said flatly. And they drove into town in silence.

On the seat beside his mother was a large basket of home-cooked food for Abner—enough for the whole weekend. In one corner of the wagon, tucked under the corn so that Mavis would not see it, was a gunnysack with Abner's money: six thousand in cash, twelve bundles of twenty-five twenty-dollar bills.

"I'll drop you off at the jail with Pa's food," Billy said. "Once the corn is ground, I'll come by."

"Are you sure?"

"Sure," Billy said. He smiled as if he had no worries in the world.

"He'll be hungry—you can bet on that," Mavis said, looking uptown toward the big red courthouse and the square brick jail alongside it.

Billy braked to a stop out front.

"Take your time," Mavis said to Billy. She smiled briefly. "Funny. Your father being in jail has given him and me more time to talk than I ever can remember."

"That's good, Ma." Billy glanced at the town clock.

"I mean real conversation. Without any interruptions—the cows, the chickens, the fields. Neither of us has any excuse not to just sit and talk to each other."

"Fine, Ma," Billy said.

She eyed him with slight suspicion. "And you, Billy? Anything going on with you that I should know about?"

"Not a thing," Billy lied.

"Fine," Mavis said, a touch suspiciously. "So meet me at the jail on toward noon. I've got some shopping to do, and that way you can spend some time with your father."

"Do I have to?"

Mavis arched one eyebrow at him.

"Okay, okay," Billy muttered.

At the Feedmill there were two wagons ahead of him, which was fine: Billy had to get to the bank before it closed. Retrieving the sack of cash, clutching it under his arm, Billy headed uptown. Across the street some kids were arriving at the baseball field—but baseball was the last thing on Billy's mind right now. It was not every day that he carried around six thousand in cash.

Every car that passed contained suspicious-looking characters.

Every shopkeeper glancing out to the street cast a greedy gaze on the sack.

Every tourist on the sidewalk was a potential robber in disguise.

Ahead, coming Billy's way, was old man Kapsner, a chicken farmer from north of town who occasionally brought some broken item to Abner for welding.

"Hey there, Billy," the old man said pleasantly.

Billy eyed him, then slunk across to the other side of the street.

The old man stopped to stare; he scratched his head as Billy hurried on to the bank.

First Farmers' Bank, a brick building with small windows, was a place he had never been inside. Billy stepped through the doors into soft music and cool, conditioned air. Several people glanced over at him. At his dusty bag.

The tellers were young women in skirts and blouses with high collars, dressed as if trying to appear older. Billy felt like he should be dressed up, or at least take off his cap, but he didn't. Abner had often said that bankers were nobody's friend.

Billy chose one of the prettier tellers and stepped up to the counter.

"May I help you?"

"I'd like six thousand dollars' worth of dimes."

She stared at him (she had fine teeth and wore perfume)—then laughed. "Now really, what can I do for you today?"

Billy lifted the dusty sack onto the counter. "I'd like six thousand dollars' worth of dimes. I have the cash here."

Her eyes flickered to the side, to an older lady, then to a small camera mounted high up in the corner.

"Hello, anything I can do?" the older woman said to Billy. DOLORES GELDERSLEEVE, HEAD

TELLER, her name tag read. She had a fixed smile that reminded Billy of Mrs. Sanders, the social worker who had grilled him (and who was coming to the farm sometime soon this summer).

"This young man wants to exchange cash for six thousand dollars' worth of dimes."

The head teller's smile remained unchanged.

"That's right," Billy said.

"Do you have an account here?"

"My family does," Billy said.

"Name?"

"Baggs. Abner Baggs."

The head teller nodded slightly to the younger teller, who turned to a file drawer and expertly fingered her way through the files till she pulled one out.

"Yes. Here we are," the younger woman said.

The head teller frowned. "A new account. Opened May second—with one dollar."

She turned to Billy.

He kept his face blank and expressionless.

"A savings account with one dollar in it," she repeated.

Billy waited.

"And you want to do what?"

Billy untied the bag and began to lay out the piles of money. Some oat dust had turned the green bills slightly white, and Billy blew away the dust as he counted.

The young teller's eyes widened.

The older teller sneezed.

"There it is," Billy said at length. "All six thousand."

"Well, certainly we don't—right now at least—have six thousand dollars' worth of dimes on hand."

"You don't?" Billy said. "I thought this was a bank."

"Well, of course it's a bank," the head teller said, trying to maintain her fake smile.

"So I'd like my dimes."

The head teller stared at him. "One moment please." She went to the side of the bank, where there were two offices with glass picture windows. One of the offices read FULTON GALLOWAY, PRESIDENT.

Billy watched as the bank president listened to the head teller. Twice she held up her arms as if in disbelief. Not once did the balding Galloway change his expression or look out into the bank; for some reason that impressed Billy.

Soon enough the head teller returned. There was color in her neck, and her lips pursed themselves like the mouth of an old sucker fish.

"Mr. Galloway says if you will leave your cash here on deposit, he will order the dimes from the treasury in Saint Paul. Other than that, there's no problem."

The younger teller held back a smile.

Billy eyed the money. Abner's money. "I have to leave the money here?"

"On deposit. We will of course give you a

receipt." The head teller beamed her strongest fake smile Billy's way.

Billy thought about that. "How long will it take? To get the dimes?"

"Your dimes should be here in a week or so. May we let you know?" the head teller said.

"Sure," Billy said pleasantly.

That off his mind—at least for a few days—Billy headed back to the Feedmill. On the way he stopped by Gene's Market and bought a tin of RedMan Chewing Tobacco and a pack of bubble gum. He consider buying a pack of baseball cards but didn't. It was a stupid habit of Tiny Tim Loren's, spending so much cash on cards. Tim had well over three thousand cards now; no wonder the kid had to see a shrink once a week.

Tucking a wad of RedMan into his cheek, Billy headed back to the Feedmill.

And the baseball field.

In a small town such as Flint, nearly everything was in sight. The school sat just up the block from the mill, and the baseball field lay nearly straight across from the dusty, humming building where farmers came and went with their wagons and trucks. From a distance, Billy could see that the line for the corn grinder had not moved forward much, and so there was time for him to stop by the field. The town team had assembled now, and Coach Anderson was cracking balls around the infield and outfield. His voice echoed across the field.

"One out, runners at the corners—where's the play?"

"Two out, runners on second and third, infield up—where's the play?"

"Nobody out, runners at first and second, ground ball to short—where's the play?"

"You mean me?" Billy heard Tim shout from right field.

"Short—short," the coach called.

"I am short," Tiny Tim called.

Billy shook his head; some things never changed.

Off to the side, King Kenwood threw from the warm-up mound in his smooth, wheeling, right-handed delivery. Billy watched him. For some reason Kenwood stopped and looked around. Looked Billy's way. Then he turned back to the mound and delivered his pitch, which popped hard into Butch Redbird's glove.

Back at the mill, Billy waited in the pickup as an older man stiffly, slowly climbed into his truck, then fumbled with the gear shift. Billy slammed the truck seat with his cap and swore to himself. "You stupid old bastard, I haven't got all day."

Finally the farmer inched his wagon out the other side, and Billy drove forward onto the scale and dump hopper. He braked the wagon just ahead of a square, grated hole in the floor. Billy hopped out as the miller weighed the truck and wagon.

"Okay," the dusty man called as he wrote

down the weight. Billy jerked open the wagon's gate and began the flood of ears and oats into the floor grate. Below, the big grinders slowly started to hum, like an airplane taking off, louder and louder. Billy emptied the wagon in record time, clanging its steel sides with his shovel, even sweeping out the wagon's corners. He did things differently—better—when he was in charge.

"Add a hundred fifty pounds of soybean meal, ten salt and three mineral," Billy called to the miller.

The dusty miller looked up, surprised. "Your old man usually takes just the salt."

Billy glared at the man. "I don't see my old man around here, do you?"

"No," the miller said evenly, "I was just—"

"Just give me the hundred fifty soy."

The miller shrugged and began to weigh out the soybean meal.

Billy went out into the Feedmill to cool off. For some unexplained reason he disliked the miller, a bearded dust bunny only a few years older than Billy and already married with a couple of kids. He had to be real stupid or else a real loser to work at a Feedmill. Stupid, probably. What was so difficult about adding a hundred fifty pounds of soybean meal?

Billy wanted the soybean supplement for a nonstupid reason. The last year or so he had been reading the *Dairy Science Newsletter* from the University of Minnesota Ag Campus. It came in the mail free, though Abner usually threw the newsletter in the burner barrel with a comment like "I know my own damn cows and I sure as hell don't need some scientist in a white coat telling me what to do." But Billy sometimes rescued the newsletters before they burned. And now that Abner was in jail, Billy had plenty of time to mull over what the dairy scientists were saying: Dairy cows needed extra protein during early lactation. That was to say, right after a cow calved, and when she was milking heavily, the cow needed more than just corn, oats and hay. A protein supplement like soybean meal (which was almost twenty percent protein) paid off three to four times in increased milk production.

"There's all kinds of ways to part a fool and his money," Abner would surely say to that idea, but right now Billy was in charge, and he didn't need any stupid, dusty miller telling him he wasn't.

On the way back to the jail, Billy drove the truck and wagon past the ball field. In the shade he coasted to a stop and let the engine idle. He paused there, watching the town kids field and throw the ball. From under the truck seat he fished a pack of cigarettes and lit one. He sat there smoking, watching. He could see why men smoked. Cigarettes had something to do with the hands and with anger: A person could not make a fist while he was holding a cigarette.

"Hey, Billy!" someone shouted. It was Tiny

Tim; he was always looking around, paying attention to everything except the play at hand.

All the players, and the coach, too, turned to look.

"Time," the coach called quickly, and began to jog over to the truck.

Billy jammed the cigarette into his mouth, the truck into gear, and drove off with a jerk. He did not look back.

Billy parked a half block from the jail, then sat and finished his cigarette. Afterward he popped the bubble gum into his mouth and trudged up the street toward the squat, square brick building. His feet clumped up the sharp granite steps; at the top he took a deep breath, then went inside. At the front desk he stopped before a stern-looking woman jailor.

"Abner Baggs?" she said, not looking up. "Yes, he's here. Why wouldn't he be?"

"I dunno, I thought maybe he'd be out on the work crew," Billy mumbled.

"The work crew is out, but your father was a bad boy and has to stay inside. Something about him scaring off some tourists down at City Park."

"Can I go on back to see him?"

"He has a visitor right now."

"That's my ma with him."

She peered up at him. "You sixteen? Gotta be sixteen to go back there unaccompanied."

"I'm sixteen," Billy said, stretching up slightly.

She gave him an extra-long glare. "Okay, go on back."

As she looked back at her papers, Billy gave the crabby old fart a flying middle finger.

Billy passed along the cells. Though he kept his eyes straight ahead, he could see men on both sides, one snoring on his iron cot, another watching a little black-and-white television. "Shay kid," an old man rasped drunkenly at Billy, "shay—come here for a second, kid."

Billy kept moving. Many of the cells were empty.

In the last cell on the left were Abner and Mavis. He paused before the iron bars. Inside, his mother sat leaning against his father; Abner had his arm stiffly around her, and he was staring off through his little window.

"Promise me you'll stay out of any more trouble," Mavis was saying.

Abner was silent.

"Langen will keep you inside here for the whole sentence. At least on the work crew you can get some fresh air."

"I just . . . sometimes the sight of some people," Abner said, "like those tourists . . . they just . . . set me off. They just—"

Abner looked up suddenly. "Billy!" he said sharply.

Mavis straightened up immediately. Her eyes were reddened, and she wiped at them with the back of her hand.

"Sorry, Pa," Billy began, "I didn't mean . . . I wasn't spyin' on you."

"It's all right," Mavis said quickly. "There's no real door to knock on, is there?" She tried to make it a joke, but her voice faltered. She stood up and tidied her dress. "You can chat with your father for a while while I finish my grocery shopping. I'll stop back in a while. A half an hour?"

"I need to get the wagon home and unloaded," Billy said.

"Twenty minutes, then," his mother said. The cell door was unlocked, and she opened it for Billy. "I'll hurry right back."

And then it was just Billy and Abner.

"Step in," his father said. "Pull up an easy chair."

Billy eased inside the bare cell; he inspected the iron bars, the window.

"Too small for a man to fit through," Abner said, watching Billy.

Billy's eyes strayed to the toilet, which was a lidless, battered stainless-steel cup that stuck up from the floor in the corner of the cell.

"No moving parts, and colder on your ass than a snow shovel in January."

"Least you got a TV," Billy said, looking up at the tiny set in the corner. He wished they had one at home.

"I won't watch the damn thing," Abner said. "It's just talk, talk, talk all the time. Nothing gets done. It's all talk."

Billy shrugged. He leaned against the door so he could see out, down the hall to the front. They were silent. "Where's the chief?" Billy asked. "Mr. Wind."

"Out on a work crew."

Billy nodded. They were quiet. "You shouldn't have scared off them tourists, Pa."

Abner smiled.

So did Billy a little.

"Anyway," Abner ventured, "how are things in the barn?"

"Good, good," Billy said.

"That north pasture still look good?"

"Very good," Billy said.

Silence came again to the cell.

"Are you keepin' up all right? With the work, I mean."

"Sure," Billy said.

"The calf pens? The chicken coop?"

"Yes—I told you, yes."

Abner nodded. He leaned back on his bunk. "How about Skinner? How's that old mutt?"

Billy felt something loosen up inside him, felt part of him relax. "Same old stuff with him, keeping the barn cats in line and sleeping in the shade."

His father nodded pleasantly enough. Then he squinted slightly at Billy. "Seen any of the neighbors recently?"

"Not really."

Abner picked at a fingernail, then looked up. "Somebody said they saw you and them Erickson girls down at Bob's Barn."

Billy swallowed. "I drove down to get a pop, that was all."

"And took them along?"

Billy nodded.

"Don't do it again," Abner said.

Billy said nothing.

"I don't want you hangin' around with those two," Abner said. "Your ma don't like it and I don't like it."

"They're not the worst girls in the world."

"That oldest one, Heather, just had somebody's kid. That tells me something about her."

Billy shrugged.

"Girls like that are too fast. First thing you know—"

"I know, I know," Billy said sharply.

"Do you? What do you know about girls?"

"Enough," Billy said lamely, and looked down at his boots.

"Your ma and I just want to make sure you do," Abner said. "We don't want to see any little Erickson kid that's long and blue-eyed and left-handed."

"For God's sakes, Pa!"

"All right, all right—your ma's seen that little bastard and it's clear he don't have anything to do with us—but I'm just tryin' to keep you out of trouble."

"Keep me out of trouble? Me?" Billy said angrily, gesturing with both hands at the jail cell.

Abner raised the back of his hand as if to

whack Billy a good one. But then he pursed his lips, lowered his arm. He let his own eyes travel, slowly, about the jail cell.

Billy was silent. "Pa, I didn't mean—"

"No, you were right." His father looked back at Billy, and his shoulders jumped with a short laugh.

Billy grinned.

Soon both of them were laughing loudly.

"Wash sho goddamn funny over there?" the drunk in the next cell shouted.

"Shut up, you old bastard!" Abner shouted back pleasantly, and he and Billy kept laughing like fools.

Mavis, returned from shopping, reappeared at the cell door. "Goodness," she said, "what in the world can be so funny?"

This set Billy and Abner to hooting all over again.

Monday morning, after the early milking and then breakfast, Billy buried himself in his work. Back in the barn he cleaned the gutter and cow platform. He scraped and limed the concrete floor, then forked over all of it a fluffy blanket of fresh, yellow straw—clean bedding for the cows.

As he worked, the cloudy, overcast day showed cement gray in the small windows of the barn. Billy reached upward to the nearest light bulb; he wiped away the dust and grime.

Only forty watts.

He checked the next bulb. Forty watts again.

"No wonder it's so damn dim in here," he said to Skinner, and set down his fork. First he took a bucket of soapy water and splashed the windows. They were clouded with fly specks and dust, and it took hard scrubbing to get the panes clear and chirpy clean. After that, Billy wiped each light bulb as clean as the window glass. Then he found a stack of aluminum-foil pie tins in Mavis's pantry; in each one he cut a hole, then tacked it to the barn ceiling around each light fixture, making a reflector for each bulb. It was a trick he had read about in the *Dairy Science Newsletter*. Lastly he went down the row and switched on each light; with every bulb, the interior of the old barn seemed to widen a foot and its ceiling to lift two feet. He stood back to admire his handiwork. "There," he said to Skinner, "what was so hard about that?"

In the afternoon he mucked out the calf pen, limed it, bedded the clean-smelling floor with straw. While the floor was now fresh and bright, the walls, battered and stained from years of calves, looked all the worse.

With a bucket, five pounds of lime and two quarts of water (Billy had read the recipe in the *Dairy Science Newsletter*) Billy made cheap white barn paint. With a broom he smeared the runny, chalky mixture on the walls. The calves huddled in the corner, confused at the sharp, clean smell. When he had finished painting, the pen walls looked mainly wet—and still old and dark. Discouraged, Billy splashed the remainder of the lime paint on the darkest spots, then headed outside, where the sun had begun to shine.

Skinner waited with his ball.

"Hey, boy," Billy said tiredly. He gave Skinner a few halfhearted tosses, then sat with him in the sunshine alongside the hay shed. He realized he had been working since five in the morning; it was now after four o'clock in the afternoon.

On the south side of the hay shed the sun was

warm, like a yellow blanket falling on him, and he lay back on the bales. The sunlight slowly radiated through his skin and right into his bones. . . .

The next thing he knew, Skinner was barking and someone was calling his name.

He sat up, rubbed his face. His mother was hurrying forward, home already from work.

"Billy—I saw you lying there. . . . For a second you scared me!"

Billy jumped up, disoriented; his mother's face was chalky white. "I was just . . . Skinner and I were . . ."

Mavis looked relieved. "Don't be afraid of a little nap if you need one," Mavis said. Then her eyes traveled down his shirt to his pants to his old boots.

"Look at you," Mavis said. Her voice caught.

Billy glanced down. It was true: He had forgotten to wear coveralls today. His jeans and shirt and boots were spotted with manure splash and dirt and white lime.

"You can't work this hard all summer," Mavis said, her eyes turning worried at their corners. "I told Abner it was too much. . . ."

"I can do it," Billy answered immediately. "Come look at the barn." He was fully awake by now.

She followed him inside. He switched on the lights.

"Well!" she said, flabbergasted. "I've never

seen it look so . . . white . . . so clean. So good."
She turned. "And the pens, too!"

Billy turned also. The watery lime paint had
dried to a flat, full white, and the little black-
and-white calves kicked and bounded about,
throwing up sprays of fresh straw as if they were
at a wild party in a new house.

"Your father would be very proud," Mavis
said.

Billy shrugged.

"He would," Mavis said.

"Maybe," Billy allowed.

"Well, I know I am," his mother said. She
leaned closer as if to hug him, then, with another
glance at his clothes, and a wrinkling of her nose,
thought the better of it. "I'll get changed and
help with milking."

"You don't have to," Billy said, but in truth he
was glad for the company.

After chores, the dairy cows were turned out
of their stanchions to pasture where they would
graze and doze all night; then Billy washed up the
milker and himself along with it, and finally he
and his mother headed to the house for supper.

Suppers were different now. They were looser,
more relaxed, longer. Tonight as they ate maca-
roni hot dish and bread and pickles and apple-
sauce, Mavis talked about the Doctors' Clinic,
about the nurses there, about Doctor Lloyd. She
often talked about Doctor Lloyd, about the amus-
ing things he said, about his easy way with the

continually bickering nurses, his civilized manners.

Billy talked about his idea for the dairy cows, the soybean meal and its extra protein.

"Why not try it?" Mavis said. "Though your father . . ."

"He'll never know," Billy answered. "At the Feedmill I worked out a deal—a wagon full of corn for the soybean meal, enough to last all summer."

Mavis smiled. "You're a good little farmer."

Billy bent to his pie.

"Maybe too good," she added.

Billy looked up.

She kept staring at him. "After supper you want to play catch?"

"With you?" Billy asked.

"Sure," Mavis said.

"Okay!" Billy said, wolfing down the last bite.

"But dishes first," Mavis said sternly. "You wash. Your hands and arms could use some more soap and water."

Later, with a tawny yellow sun hung in the west, Billy and Mavis headed into the yard. Across the fence, the herd of Holsteins rested in the big pasture like a school of great black-and-white fish in a green sea; the cows' noses all pointed in the same direction, into the faint southern breeze, and their tails switched away flies in a continuous swimming motion. Closer in, the chickens picked at leftover grain or else sat fluffed up and contented in the sunlight. The only living thing on the farm not relaxed and slightly sleepy was Skinner. At the sight of the baseball gloves and ball he began to bark and race in wild circles.

"Here, boy," Billy said. With the old rubber ball he demonstrated Skinner's skills to Mavis, who laughed and got into the game herself. She could throw the ball almost as far as Billy.

Finally, when Skinner was pooped, Billy tied him up; otherwise, he would have killed himself chasing after barn-rule doubles. Then Billy and his mother began to play catch.

"An orange baseball," Mavis said, rolling it in her fingers. "Where'd you get an orange baseball?"

"From Coach Anderson."

"I should have guessed."

The bright ball looped back and forth. Billy made sure not to throw too hard. He also helped his mother with her form.

"When you throw, put your glove hand way out, then follow through with your throwing arm," Billy coached. "It gives you better balance that way." Mavis was left-handed, like Billy. "Also, get more of your legs into it."

Her throws got straighter, harder. From her garden work she had always had strong arms and hands and fingers.

"You're pretty good," Billy said. "You could be on a team."

Mavis shrugged. "They never had teams, or

sports at all for girls, when I went to school," she said, rifling the ball back to Billy.

"None?" Billy said, pausing to hold the ball.

She shook her head sideways. "Cheerleading of course. And phys. ed., which was mainly jumping rope and social dance. That was all."

The orange baseball lofted back and forth.

"Now in school there are lots of sports for girls," Billy said.

"But not enough," Mavis said. "I say when it comes to sports, there ought to be equal time for boys and girls."

"A girls' football team? A girls' baseball team?" Billy scoffed.

"During World War II there were women's professional baseball teams—a whole league of them."

Billy looked skeptically at his ma.

"It's true," Mavis said.

Billy listened; they kept tossing the ball.

"All the men were gone off to war, so the women started a league."

"Weird," Billy said.

"Not really, when you think about it."

Billy tossed the ball back. "Were they any good?"

"Sure they were."

"As good as the men?"

"Good in different ways. So I'd say yes, they were as good as the men's teams," Mavis replied. "And very popular."

"If they were so popular, what happened to them?"

"The war ended." Mavis held the ball. She looked at it in her hand. "When the war ended, the men came home and took back their game." Then she arced the baseball back to Billy. For a while they tossed the ball in higher, almost thoughtful throws, then began to bear down and put some speed on it.

"I still say you could be on a team," Billy said.

Mavis smiled. Abruptly she held the ball and stared across at Billy. "So why don't we start one?"

Billy looked across to his ma.

"A team of our own," she said.

"There's only two of us," Billy said, gesturing for the ball.

"Three, counting Skinner," Mavis said.

Skinner perked up his ears briefly at his name, then slipped back to sleep.

"Seriously. Why not?" Mavis said, walking toward Billy, rolling the orange ball in her big hands, thinking all the while. "We could round up some neighbors. Start a team."

"Neighbors? Like who?" The closest neighbors were the Erickson girls; Ole Svendson, a painfully shy bachelor farmer; and Big Danny Boyer, a giant, silent farm kid.

"You might be surprised at who'd come out to play ball."

Billy found himself holding the orange baseball. "If we got up a team, who would we play?"

"I'm not sure. I supposed we'd worry about that later."

From close range they tossed the ball back and forth a couple of more times.

"Are you serious about this?" Billy ventured. "About starting a farm team?"

"'Farm Team,'" Mavis said. "I like the name."

She wound up and rifled a throw that stung Billy's glove hand. She stood there and smiled at him. "Sure I'm serious. Who's to stop us?"

O n Tuesday Mavis returned from work
carrying a stack of fliers. "Designed and
typed by yours truly," she said, handing
one to Billy.

Billy read the announcement:

> *All Work and No Play?*
> *Announcing*
> *BASEBALL!*
> *Friday Nights (weather permitting)*
> *at the Abner Baggs Farm*
> *17 mi. west, 3 mi. north of Flint*
> *(Township Road #11, RFD #272)*
> *after chores until dark.*
> *BASEBALL!*
> *Come one, come all. . . .*

"It looks good Ma, but . . ."

"But what?"

"We don't have a field."

"What do you mean, 'We don't have a field'?
This is a farm—we've got plenty of fields."

The pasture just west of the barn was perfect. Well, not perfect, but it was mostly flat, and the grass was clipped short by the grazing Holsteins. Of course the big cows left their pies here and there, and around each dung pile the grass grew like a hairy, green wart on the field—but with a shovel and scythe those could be taken care of. There were a few gopher mounds, too, but Billy had traps. There was no outfield fence—yet. And of course a pitcher's mound was needed.

The next evening Billy and Mavis hurried through supper in order to get started. For both agreed on one thing: They would not distribute the baseball fliers until the field was ready.

In the pasture their first task was to remove the cow pies. His mother drove the little H Farmall tractor, and Billy forked the dung into the manure spreader hooked behind. Mavis *chug-chugged* the tractor in slow, steady circles about the field. The Holsteins, curious, ambled in from the far pasture to look—and, as they stood around gawking, they humped up their backs and began to leave new, steaming piles.

"Stop that—get—hiee, hiee!" Billy shouted, shooing the lumbering Holsteins back toward the far pasture. Mavis helped herd the cows by driving the tractor close behind them and shouting, and even Skinner got into the act.

After the cow pies were finally gone, Billy

brought around the scythe. Swinging the long-handled blade, he trimmed the high grass spots. Then they began to measure out the diamond, using a spool of baler twine. Billy drove a small wooden stake at home plate.

Another stake for first base.

But second base was harder to pinpoint. They had to do some serious figuring on a sheet of paper in order to get the diamond exactly square. Mavis took the opportunity to sermonize about the value of math, of geometry.

"Right, Ma," Billy mumbled.

Then third base.

And back to home plate.

"What about the bases themselves?" Billy said.

"I've got an idea for them," Mavis said. "I'll work on them tomorrow night."

"I'll take care of the mound," Billy said.

"But not tonight, no more work tonight."

"Aw, come on, Ma!"

"We've done enough for one night," Mavis said firmly.

Billy didn't argue further. The sun was long gone behind the horizon, and pale wisps of ground fog had begun to creep in and cotton the lowest area in right field. "A baseball field's a lot of work," Billy admitted as they trudged toward the house.

"Just what we didn't need." Mavis smiled.

"But it's fun work."

She put her hand on his shoulder.

They walked along in silence. "Do you think anybody will come?" Billy asked.

"Sure they will," Mavis said without a second thought.

Billy was silent for a few steps. "You know why, probably?"

"Because we have the best baseball field around," Mavis said.

"No. They'll come mainly because they know Pa's not here."

Mavis stopped short to look at him, then at the field. Her eyes began to glisten. "Come on," she said, steering him toward the house. "I'll make us some hot chocolate."

The next day, Thursday, between milking and barn chores and getting the corn cultivator ready, Billy worked more on the baseball field. One big problem was the cows; they had come back during the night and pooped all over the infield plus trampled Billy's stakes.

Billy hauled in the rolls of brown snow fencing and began to unwind them. Snow fencing was made of thin wooden slats about two inches wide that were held in place by wires running crosswise to the slats; used in the winter to prevent snow blowing across driveways or roads, it would make for a perfect outfield fence.

Billy stepped off the distances from home plate, drove small stakes. There was plenty of room in the outfield, acres and acres of it, but Billy put straightaway center field at two hundred fifty feet, and the corners at two hundred. He did not want the field to look so large that people would be scared off by it. With a sledgehammer he began to drive steel posts.

The sharp *ting-ting-ting!* attracted the Holsteins, of course. They drifted in from the pasture to see what was going on and began to sniff, then rub against the posts. Their 1200-pound bulks began to bend some of the posts.

"Get back! Hiee! You devils," Billy shouted.

They backed off only slightly. Stretchy came up closest to Billy and stuck out her long, pink, rough tongue. Billy relented, and paused to knuckle-rub her long snout. "There. Now beat it, Stretchy!" he said. "Can't you see I'm working?"

"Mooo!" she answered, and showed her old yellow teeth. "Moo . . ." Luckily she led the herd back toward the barn, to the dusty lot where the flies were not so pesky and where the water tank stood.

An hour later Billy was sweating hard but the snow fencing was wired in place. He headed back to home plate, then looked out at the curving fence. The ball field had shape now; that was what fences did—they gave shape to things. With an imaginary bat he took a few practice swings.

The mound required some thought. He considered its distance from home plate. Regulation distance was sixty feet six inches. Little League was forty-five feet six inches. He had no idea who might show up to be on the Farm Team, so what if he split the difference? The difference was . . . fifteen feet. Half of that was seven and a half. That added up to fifty-three feet. . . . He scratched numbers in the dirt with a stick.

Subtracted.

Divided.

Added.

Mavis was right, of course: Math kept popping up when he least expected it, especially with baseball and farming.

Fifty-three feet. That was his answer. He measured it exactly and stood there facing the home-plate area. The distance felt just right.

Climbing aboard the tractor, with Skinner riding in the empty front scoop, Billy headed down the lane to the old gravel hole. It was where he target shot his deer rifle before the fall season, and his little .22 anytime. As he drove along, the breeze felt good on his face and inside his shirt. Usually Abner operated the tractor, but not today. Usually when Billy drove the tractor, he thought at least once of Robert, of the accident—but not today. It was baseball that kept his mind moving forward, not back. . . .

At the gravel pit he scooped up a load of dirt, then headed again to the baseball field. Skinner trotted along. Billy made four trips—three scoops of gravel and one of heavier clay mixed in on top—then graded the pile to rough form with the tractor's scoop. After that he backed over the mound several times to pack it about ten inches high. Then, with a few minutes of hand raking, presto—a solid pitcher's mound.

Billy stepped onto it. He needed a pitching rubber, of course, but he would figure that out later. Right now he stared down at home plate. He went into a wind-up; threw an imaginary strike.

Which was when he heard clapping. Far off, but distinctly, he heard the sound of one person slowly clapping. He froze—looked around him.

Robert—that was his first thought. It had to be Robert, clapping slow and steady. Robert's presence filled the field as surely as if he had risen from the dark earth into which the tractor's disk had crushed him. "Robert?" Billy called hoarsely. "Robert!" He felt his knees turn weak, his breath shorten up; goose bumps washed across his arms and down his back as the hollow, thudding sound continued.

Then he saw Stretchy close to the barn, switching her tail. With each quick swing, the tail smacked against the wood.

Thud.

Thud.

Thud.

Thud.

Billy let out a groan as if he had been hit in the gut by a fastball; he sank to his knees in the fresh dirt of the pitcher's mound. He knelt there, holding his shoulders, his face buried in his arms.

Skinner raced over and began to lick and lick Billy's face, as if trying to clean it. "I'm okay, I'm okay—" Billy kept saying. But the old dog did not give up until Billy was.

That evening after chores, with the presence of Robert still strong about the field, Billy worked on the base paths. Using white barn lime funneled through an old piece of pipe, Billy followed the twines about the diamond. Narrow white lines unwound straight behind him. As he finished, Mavis appeared carrying an armload of bases.

"Neat!" Billy said, hefting the bags. She had taken white flour sacking, sewn it into squares and stuffed them tightly with straw. When the bases were in place, Billy and Mavis sat back to admire their handiwork. The sun was just setting. The cows, bored by the goings-on, drifted back to the far pasture. The white lines of the diamond drew light from the deepening orange.

"It's a beautiful field," Mavis said.

Billy was silent.

"Don't you think?" she said turning to Billy.

"I . . . thought Robert was here today," he murmured. He had not planned to say anything about it. About the clapping. About the goose bumps on his arms.

Mavis blinked back the new water in her eyes. "Of course he was here," Mavis said, pulling Billy closer. "Why wouldn't he be?"

They headed to the house in silence. The

whole farm felt lonely. First Robert, now his pa was gone. At the porch steps, with the last of the sunlight striking low, like an orange flood across the farm, they both sat down to take one more look.

"One time," Billy began, "during the fall when Pa had Robert climb the silo to get the door open for silo filling, I wanted to climb it, too. . . ." Speaking softly, looking across the farm to the high dome of the silo, he told her the story—

Of waiting until Robert was back down from the forty-foot climb, until he was occupied with other work (their father was far off in the field on his tractor). Of scrambling up the short wooden ladder to reach the first rungs of the silo's skinny steel ladder, which did not reach all the way to the ground for that very reason—to prevent kids from climbing it. Of scrambling quickly up the thin iron rungs—trying to get as high as he could before Robert spotted him.

But Robert did not spot him. In less than two minutes Billy was all the way to the top, to the little steel crow's nest. He had seen Robert push its floor upward with his head, had seen Robert pull himself inside and let the platform swing back down to become a real floor (it swung only one way); Billy did the same thing.

Suddenly he was secure and safe atop the silo's perch. He turned to face the farm and the land—and the breath whooshed out of him. Far off he could see the glint of Stump Lake—which was five miles away! He could see his father on the tractor near the far-west fence line, plowing oat stubble on a side hill, the curving strip of yellow field turning black behind him slower than the minute hand turning on a clock. In the middle of their farm was the black-green cedar swamp with patches of gray water; and closer in was the sawmill with its dull mounds of sawdust. Directly below were silage wagons and a tractor—all no bigger than toys. The chickens in their yard seemed as small as snowflakes, and when Skinner trotted by, they scattered in a swirl of tiny white particles.

Billy whistled. Skinner skidded to a stop and looked around.

Billy laughed and whistled again. Skinner's head flopped from side to side as he tried to locate Billy— which was when Robert came running from the machine shed. He knew immediately where Billy was.

"Get down from there right now!"

"Don't have to!"

"You heard me—right now!"

Billy laughed and spit at Robert—but the breeze whirled it away.

Shading his eyes, Robert stared up at Billy. Then he checked his wristwatch. "All right," he called, looking back skyward. "Stay up there then. Come down when you're ready."

"Okay, I will," Billy said defiantly, and leaned back to enjoy the view.

This lasted only a few minutes. The air was surprisingly chilly up that high. Billy counted the steps back down: thirty-five of them. He examined the platform. How, he wondered, did it lift up so he could get back onto the ladder?

"So how is it up there?" Robert called as he passed across the yard carrying some tools; he made a point of not looking up.

"It's just fine," Billy said, and tried to spit at him again.

Robert went out of sight into the machine shed. Billy could hear him pounding on something in there.

"Robert?" he called.

Robert took a long time coming out. "What!" he said crabbily.

"How does the platform lift up?"

"Use your left foot, then put your right one on the first rung."

Billy was silent.

"Well, go ahead and do it!" Robert said. He had come closer now, straight underneath the ladder.

"Like this?" Billy said. His voice was slightly shaky.

"Just like that," Robert said. He let his hammer drop to the ground as he kept looking up, kept giving instructions.

Billy was silent now. The wind seemed to increase; he felt it cold inside his shirt. The muscles in his legs began to tremble.

"What's a matter?" Robert called.

"Nothing," Billy managed to say.

"So stay up there, then," Robert said, and began to walk slowly back to the machine shed.

Billy watched him go. He kept watching the open shed door through which Robert had disappeared. His eyes were tearing now, partly because of the wind, partly because . . . When he saw Robert peep around the corner to check on him, Billy wailed, "Robert—I can't get down!"

"You got up there, you can get down."

"I can't, Robert, I can't. . . ."

"If I come get you, will you promise not to be stupid ever again?"

"I promise," Billy blubbered.

"Obey me forever and ever," Robert added.

"Yes—forever."

"And clean the calf pen for me next Saturday?" Robert grinned. His teeth shone whiter than bone.

"Yes! Yes!" Billy wailed.

Within seconds the silo's iron ladder rang sharply with the sound of Robert's boots. "Stand to the side while I push up the platform," he instructed.

Billy shut his eyes and followed orders; Robert was just below him.

"Now wrap your legs around my neck."

Billy did so immediately.

"Jesus! Not so hard!" Robert croaked. "You're choking me."

Billy let up slightly.

"Hang on to the rungs just like you did coming up," Robert advised. "One by one, that's how you do it," he murmured. "One step at a time."

And then, quickly, Billy clamped atop Robert's shoulders, they were down.

Billy wiped his teary face with two fists. "You're gonna tell Pa," he said with certainty.

Robert laughed loud and clear, with an echo off the

barn. "Tell? Why would I tell now that I have a slave forever?"

"Not forever," Billy said stubbornly.

"Forever," Robert said. "That's what you agreed to." He laughed again and faked a couple of punches at Billy's runny nose.

"How do I get to be not your slave?" Billy asked, his shoulders still jerking with an intermittent hic-coughing sob.

Robert grinned. His blue eyes flashed like the patch on a teal's wing; his smile was brighter than July sun at noon. "Simple," he said. "You've got to climb the silo again. All the way up and all the way down— by yourself."

In the present there was a long, electric moment. "Well?" Billy's mother whispered. "Did you?"

Billy nodded yes.

They sat there quietly; the sun was gone now, and darker blue was beginning to fall in on top of the horizon. When Billy looked back again, his mother was weeping. He put his arm around her. They sat there several minutes. "I've got an idea, Ma," he said. "How about if we head down to Bob's for a root beer, and deliver some mail along the way?"

With Skinner along for the ride, and the deer easing out of the timber to graze at the edges of fields, and the blue twilight falling to purple, Billy drove the country roads and Mavis stuffed baseball fliers into mailboxes.

Miles and miles of graveled, dusty back roads they drove.

Roads, in the twilight, that Billy did not recall ever being on.

Roads narrow and rutted, where cows snorted and shied from the fence.

Roads close between darkening groves of trees, where hunting owls flapped and glided.

Roads winding uphill and down, where the farms were miles apart and lonely mailboxes, aluminum colored and half round, began to rise up in the dark like new moons. Into each went a baseball flier: "Come one, come all. . . ."

Now there was only the waiting. Friday dawned clear and warm, and the sky slowly lightened from robin's egg to a paler blue. During morning milking Billy checked the barn clock every few minutes. The clock hands crawled as slow as a daddy longlegs in winter.

After breakfast he lay underneath the corn cultivator, making some final adjustments on the shields. Abner's corn, having escaped the frost, was already a long hand high, and the weeds were coming up fast. As Billy worked, Skinner wooted. On the driveway gravel scraped and bike fenders clattered. Billy looked up to see Gina Erickson approaching at full speed.

"Hey, Billy," she called, waving the flier like a flag, "what the hell's this?"

"Can't you read?" Billy said, returning to his work. He cranked the wrench.

Gina hopped off her bike and let it fall with a crash. "'Announcing baseball! Friday nights at the Abner Baggs farm . . . Come one, come all.' Does that mean girls and everybody?"

"My ma wrote it," Billy said, "so I guess it does."

"Far out," Gina said brightly. Then she frowned. "I don't have no glove."

"So you can be a cheerleader."

"I don't want to be no damn cheerleader—I want to play."

Billy shrugged. "Or scorekeeper, or be on the grounds crew."

"I'm playin'," Gina said stubbornly. "What do you think I'd be best at, first base or middle field?"

"'Middle field'?" Billy squinted up through the iron curves of the cultivator. "What the hell is 'middle field'?"

"That's the outfielder in the middle."

"It's called center field," Billy said, shaking his head. "And anyway, I think center is taken." He wished she would be content to watch.

"Taken? By who?"

"That's for me to know and you to find out," Billy said.

"Who made you coach?"

"Me," Billy said.

Gina called him something unprintable.

"Watch your mouth, twerp!"

She laughed at Billy, then raced over to the diamond. Billy sat up all the way. He checked the sun, then watched her race over to the field. Soon enough he dusted himself off and followed her.

Gina stood in the infield, her mouth hanging open. "Wow! White lines, a pitcher's hill and everything."

"Pitcher's mound," Billy said.

Gina didn't hear him. "It's like a real baseball field!"

"It *is* a baseball field," Billy said.

"And there's gonna be a million people come," Gina said.

"I doubt that," Billy replied.

"We'll need bleachers. Heather and I can sell popcorn and sloppy joes. We'll make a ton of money!"

"I thought you were playing middle field."

"That's right—I forgot," Gina said. "Then Heather can run the concession stand."

"Concession stand?"

"That one—right there," Gina said, pointing.

"The corncrib?" It was a long, high, narrow building made of poles and slatted wooden sides so air could pass through it and dry the ears of corn; right now, in early summer, the crib was nearly empty.

"Sure. It's got a roof. Just take off a couple of side boards, nail a couple of planks for a counter and it would be perfect."

"You're crazy," Billy muttered. He shook his head and turned back to the tractor and his work.

"No I ain't," Gina called, picking up her bike. "You wait—a million people are gonna come."

152

After Gina was out of sight down the road, Billy sat up and looked again at the old corncrib.

At the empty diamond.

When Mavis returned home from work that afternoon, she brought more fliers. "On my lunch hour I took some around town," she said. "To the Feedmill. To the hardware stores, Gary's Welding, the John Deere dealership—those kinds of places. Tonight's the night!" Mavis said.

Billy looked at the empty baseball field.

He had fed grain to the dairy cows an hour early, at three thirty, and was done milking at five. Mavis and he ate supper at five thirty, a full hour ahead of usual. Twice cars passed on the road, but none pulled in.

"I was thinking," Mavis said. "I should go get Danny Boyer. His father will never bring him."

"Danny?" Billy said, wincing. Danny Boyer often helped with haying, but he was not allowed to go to town because once at the County Fair, underneath the bleachers, he'd shown his pecker to the Rademacher girl—or so she said. Mavis never believed the girl, and she was always extra nice to Big Danny. Trouble was, most kids were afraid of Big Danny.

"Where's he going to play?" Billy said skeptically.

"We'll find a spot for him."

"He'll scare off the other kids."

"If people knew Danny better, they wouldn't be afraid, would they?"

Billy was silent.

"Come one, come all, yes?" Mavis said.

Billy shrugged, then nodded.

"I'll be back in a jiffy," she continued. "You better stay in case someone comes."

So, checking the sun and the kitchen clock every few minutes, Billy sat on the front steps flipping his pocketknife, trying to make it stick, point down, in the wooden step, waiting.

And waiting.

Dust appeared on the road. Billy stared. A Ford station wagon, very old and rusted, with some gear tied on top, came along the main road. It slowed at the Baggs driveway, then continued past. Billy flipped his knife again.

When Billy looked up again, the old Ford was coming backward toward the mailbox. Then it turned up the driveway toward the yard.

Billy squinted. Most of the neighbors' cars he recognized, but not this one. There was all kinds of stuff—some old lawn chairs, three battered suitcases, a small charcoal grill without legs, and a roll of waterproof tarpaulins of various colors plus what looked like rakes and hoes.

Skinner barked, and the hackles rose along his neck.

"It's okay, boy," Billy murmured. As the lumbering old car came closer, Billy looked around. He wished his mother or father were home.

Inside the car were several very brown-skinned, dark-eyed people. They looked Indian, but different around the eyes and the shape of their cheekbones.

Billy stood up.

The car's engine died midway across the yard, allowing the old station wagon to coast the last few yards.

"Hola," the man driving said flatly. He did not smile.

"Ole? Ole Svendson?" Billy asked.

"Hola," the man said. "Hello."

Billy stood there, dumbly.

"You no speak Español?"

"Español?" Billy repeated. It sounded like some kind of tractor lubricant.

"Spanish," the man said with the same dark-eyed gaze.

"Spanish. No—no, I don't speak no Spanish." They were Mexicans, a family of Mexicans. Mouth open, Billy leaned slightly lower to look into the car. There were three kids at least, though what with smudged windows and all the junk—clothes and old toys and tools—there might have been more.

"But you speak *beisbol, sí?*" his wife said, smiling at Billy. She was pretty in a dark-eyed, tired-looking way, and had some teeth missing.

"Beisbol. Baseball?"

"Baseball, *sí,*" the man said with some impatience. One of the kids, a boy near Billy's age, leaned forward to listen.

The smiling mother held one of the baseball

fliers out the window. "We find thees in Fleent. We are looking for Baggs farm, where *beisbol* plays tonight?"

Billy's cautious frown went away. Even Skinner wagged his tail at the mother's friendly voice. "Yes. There is baseball here tonight," Billy said.

"Come won, come all?" the man asked.

"Come one, come all," Billy said, nodding. He gestured for the family to get out.

Which they did.

And did.

And did.

Six of them all together.

"I am Manuel González," the man said, "from Guadalupe, Mexico." He made no move to shake hands.

"And I am María González," said the short, very thin woman. There were brown half-moon shadows under her eyes, as if the walnut color of her pupils had haloed downward onto her cheeks. "Thees are the children. First ees Jesús." María pronounced it "Hay-*soos*."

A boy Billy's age stared at the ball field. Jesús made it a point to ignore Billy. He held a baseball glove so worn, its fingers had been stitched and re-covered several times; the leather was smoothly sewn and polished walnut brown with oil.

"And Gloria."

A girl about twelve nodded shyly to Billy.

"And Raúl."

A boy about ten stared at Billy. He seemed slightly friendlier than Jesús, and also held a glove behind his back.

"And the *bebé*, Juan Elvis." The man shrugged and rolled his eyes at the name. The mother, María, smiled slightly brighter as a toddler about three years old stumbled forward to pet Skinner, who licked his face; little Juan Elvis laughed.

"We are too soon for *beisbol* tonight?" María said, looking around.

"No. It's okay," Billy said.

"There ees time for supper?"

"Supper?"

"We have our own food—" Manuel said sharply.

"Sure, I didn't mean . . ." Billy began. "There's plenty of time for supper."

Manuel spoke rapidly in Spanish to his wife, and then to the children, who began to unload the grill and other cooking things from the roof of the station wagon. Each kid knew what to do, what to carry.

"Where ees okay to eat?" Manuel asked.

"Anywhere." Billy gestured to the whole yard.

"By the *beisbol* field?"

"Why not?" Billy said. He sat back on the step as the González family went forward to the edge of the field and began to set up their table and supper things.

Which was when Mavis and Big Danny Boyer drove back into the yard.

"Who's here?" Mavis called out to Billy as she parked the truck. There was excitement in her voice.

"Just the González family," Billy said casually, "from Mexico."

•

As Mavis went to greet the González family, Billy hung back to keep an eye on Big Danny, who remained in the back of the truck. It was where he always rode; he wouldn't sit inside, even in winter.

"What say, Danny?"

Danny didn't turn. He had a big, square face capped with a yellow bowl of a haircut, and he kept staring down the road to where he'd come from. It always took Danny about an hour to get where he'd been out of his mind, and where he was into it. Skinner hopped up alongside Big Danny, who blinked and leaned down to pet him; then Danny stared again back down the road. Skinner leaned close against Big Danny's massive leg.

"Good dog. Stay," Billy said. With Danny petting Skinner, Billy headed to the baseball diamond.

There a thin column of smoke was rising from the Gonzálezes' grill. Mavis, holding little Juan Elvis, was speaking with María. The two women were as different in size and look as was possible:

One was midget short and dark, the other lumberjack tall and fair. With Spanish and English and hand gestures, they appeared to be communicating just fine. Maybe that was because they were both mothers.

"Do you have milk?" Mavis said, making a drinking motion for Juan Elvis. "Would you like some milk? Some fresh milk?"

"*Leche*? *Gracias*, thank you," María said shyly.

Manuel frowned darkly and looked away. Jesús, who had the same angry eyes as his father, looked down and tugged at one of the knots on his glove.

"Billy, go get the Gonzálezes a jar of milk."

"Sure." He glanced back at Jesús, who would not look up.

When Billy returned with the milk, which María took eagerly, the Mexican family's grill sent up a clean, hot column of smoke. In a flat pan sizzled a very thin, dry looking cornmeal cake. "*Tortilla*," María said to Billy. Mr. González sat off to the side, smoking a thin, dark cigarette.

Billy repeated the word.

"*Maíz tortilla*." Mrs. González pointed to the long cornfield as she kept the tortilla moving from side to side in the pan.

"Corn tortilla," Billy said.

"*Sí*," María said. To the other side, Gloria was busy making more tortillas and finding a corner of the grill for a pot of black beans.

"*Ejote*."

"A-hotay."

"*Excelente*," María called. "Now you speak Español."

"Raúl," Jesús said, and jerked his head toward the baseball field.

The younger brother grabbed his baseball glove, one that looked homemade, little more than an oversize leather work glove overlaid with several layers of stitched rawhide. Their mother spoke sharply to the boys—something, Billy guessed, about not running off before supper: It was probably universal in every language. The boys fidgeted as she spoke, then raced off toward the field, flipping a ball easily between them.

"Billy? You want to go with them?" Mavis asked.

"Naw," Billy said with a shrug of his own. "Not right now." He pretended uninterest in the two González brothers by turning for a closer look at their car, at the gear on top. The hoes— five of them—caught his eyes. Their blades were worn thin and shiny and razor sharp; their short handles were worn smoother than any Billy had ever seen, even on the Baggs farm.

"Guadalupe," Mavis asked. "Where in Mexico is Guadalupe?"

"Gloria?" María said, and spoke in Spanish to her.

Gloria went to the car and retrieved a map, which she unrolled across the hood of the car. Her stubby brown finger traced south through

Texas, then across the border and farther down, to a spot a little northeast of Monterrey. "Guadalupe," she said shyly.

Both Billy and Mavis leaned down to look.

"And you are going where?" Mavis inquired.

"Crookston," Gloria González said, putting down her finger in northwestern Minnesota. "Crookston, Meeneesota."

Crookston was a well-known farming town about seventy miles from Flint, on the eastern edge of the Red River Valley, a rich farming area on the border between North Dakota and Minnesota.

"You work there?"

"In the sugar beets. For the beeg boss, Crystal Sugar," Manuel said. Something in his voice was sarcastic and angry; his wife spoke quickly in Spanish to him. Manuel did not reply.

"Crookston. It's so far from Guadalupe," Mavis said.

María nodded. "Very far, *sí*. But there ees work here. There ees no work in Guadalupe. And here the summer air ees *excelente*. Juan Elvis and Gloria . . ." She said something in Spanish that neither Mavis nor Billy understood.

Mr. González thumped his chest and pretended to cough.

"Asthma?" Mavis ventured.

"*Sí*," María said immediately. "In Mexico in summer eet ees hot, hot, hot. And very bad air comes from Monterrey."

"Bad air from the Americano factories," Mr. González added.

"Air like this—" María González said, passing her hand through the hot, smoky flame from the grill. "Air like smoke, bad air all the summertime, so we must come *norte*."

Manuel González laughed harshly. "In winter, the rich Americanos come south for *sole*, for the sun. In summer, the poor Mexicano comes north for work."

"Our family has never been to Mexico," Mavis replied. "We don't have that kind of money."

Manuel's dark eyes cut through smoke as he spoke to Mavis. "If you own land, you are rich. And someday, when the peso ees weaker still, you will come to Mexico—like all the rest."

"*No politica—*" María González said to her husband.

Mr. González replied with a burst of something definitely unpleasant.

"Come on, Billy," Mavis said. "We should let the Gonzálezes eat in peace."

"I'm sorry," María González murmured aside to Mavis. "Politics and who owns the land—these ideas are in him like the worm in tequila. My husband ees an angry man."

"I understand," Mavis said. "Believe me, I understand." For a moment the two women exchanged a long, unblinking look.

Then María stepped back to their car and returned with a small jar of dull-green, smooth, pickielike vegetables in brine. "Here. For you. Jalapeño, from Guadalupe."

"Peppers," Mavis said with pleasure. *"Gracias."*

Crossing the yard, Billy looked back to see the González family sit at the little table, bow their heads and cross themselves before they ate—all except Mr. González, who stared off across the fields.

"Man, that guy is madder about the world than even Pa," Billy observed.

"Every angry man has his reasons," Mavis murmured.

Billy looked at the battered old station wagon, its line-up of shiny hoes.

While the Gonzálezes ate, Gina and Heather Erickson (and the baby) arrived on bicycles. The baby jolted along in the wire basket on the front of Heather's bike.

"Goodness!" Mavis said, sucking in her breath, her eyes on the baby.

Both girls braked to a halt at the sight of Big Danny Boyer.

"It's okay, come on," Mavis called.

The girls looked at each other, then cautiously wheeled their bikes halfway into the yard.

"Don't be worrying about Danny," Mavis said. "That's all foolishness."

Warily the girls skirted the truck as Danny kept staring down the road.

"How's your baby?" Mavis said brightly to Heather.

Heather shrugged. "Cries." She had dark circles under her eyes.

"Babies do that," Mavis said pleasantly. "Did you decide on a name yet?"

Heather shook her head sideways.

"Hi, then, Baby," Mavis said cheerily. She rescued the infant from the bicycle basket. Momentarily she wrinkled her nose. "He needs changing. Let's go up on the porch and do it together, shall we, Heather?"

Heather shrugged again and plodded after Mavis.

"We'll run some water in the summer sink," Mavis said. "We'll get him all shined up."

"So who's that?" Gina said to Billy; she pointed toward the Gonzálezes' car.

Billy explained.

"Mexicans?" she said dubiously. "Here?" Then she grinned. "See, I told you people would come."

And so they did come, that first Friday evening of baseball at the Baggs farm, not a million people but a baker's dozen plus two.

The six Gonzálezes. Gina and Heather. Big Danny. Billy and Mavis themselves.

Shawn Howenstein, the butcher's son whom Billy knew, and whose father had a country locker plant and meat market; Shawn arrived *sput-sputting* on his little motorbike that was made mostly from lawn-mower parts.

Ole Svendson himself, the bachelor farmer

and hermit who never went anywhere, eased his pickup into the far corner of the yard and parked it in the shadow of the corncrib. He left the engine running. *"Hola."* Billy waved; he was greatly amused at his own joke—which no one else seemed to understand.

"Best to leave Ole alone," Mavis said to Billy, "or else you'll frighten him off."

"Ole's crazy," Gina said.

"Ole's not crazy," Mavis retorted, her voice always impatient with Gina, "he's just shy. It's a miracle he came at all." She looked down at Gina, who wore a skimpy T-shirt with no bra. "Some people could stand to be a little more shy."

Gina, as usual, missed the point.

One more car arrived at high speed, a small Toyota stuffed to overflowing with a burly driver in a baseball cap. "Hi, folks!" Coach Anderson called out as he skidded to a stop.

Billy swallowed. He felt bad about driving away from the town field the other day, but tonight the coach hopped out as friendly as ever.

"How you doin', Danny?" the coach said, pausing at the truck to put out his hand.

Big Danny blinked and took it; a ghost of a smile came over his face.

From the porch Mavis waved to Coach Anderson. She was holding Heather's baby upside down like she was dipping a chicken; then she returned to scrubbing the squalling child. Heather had put her hands over her ears.

"Baseball tonight, I hear," the coach said to Billy as they shook hands. The coach was always shaking hands, with everybody.

"How'd you find out?" Billy asked.

The coach licked a finger and held it up to the sky—sniffed the air. "I can smell a country baseball game from twenty miles off, maybe even thirty."

Billy grinned.

"Actually, I dropped by the Feedmill to ask about, when you might be coming to town again, and saw the flier." The coach looked at Billy. "Come one, come all?"

"Sure," Billy said. He tossed the orange baseball toward the coach, who caught it and then headed to look at the field.

Just then one other vehicle, a shiny El Camino pickup, purred up the driveway. "Heather—look!" Gina whispered.

Heather turned, then took a half step behind Mavis. Billy's mother looked quizzically at Heather, then at Dale Schwartz, who killed his engine and looked across at the ball field.

"What do you want?" Billy called.

"Billy," murmured Mavis. "Where in the world are your manners?"

Billy continued to glare at Schwartz.

"Hi, neighbors," Dale said, easing out of his half truck, half car. He was a short, dark, wiry man with a tight white T-shirt and tighter-still blue jeans; he lit a cigarette in one smooth motion and flipped the match Billy's way. "Thought I'd stop by and see what's goin' on." The smoking match landed an inch from Billy's foot—which he did not move.

"Nothin's goin' on," Gina said from behind Billy.

Dale continued his thin-lipped grin.

"Actually we're getting up a ball team," Mavis said. "Friends and neighbors and anybody who cares to come."

"That is very neighborly," Dale said. His eyes strayed behind Mavis to Heather, who now held the baby out of Dale's sight. He kept leaning to his left in order to get a look at the baby. "I ain't much of a ballplayer, but I like to watch."

"Suit yourself," Mavis said, giving Billy—who had begun to protest—a quick kick to the ankle. "Come one, come all."

"Just stay cool," Billy whispered to Heather. "He can't bother us here."

In short order the coach had organized everyone who wanted to play. He hustled them onto the field, Big Danny included. The González family looked wide-eyed at the giant bulk of Danny, whom the coach planted in left field. Danny did not seem to mind standing in left, watching things.

"Okay, okay," the coach called. "We're a few gloves short of a game, but we can practice."

From his camp stool by the fence, Mr. González watched intently.

"Jesús? What position do you like?"

"Short," Jesús said decisively.

"Raúl?"

"Second."

"Shawn?"

"Third, I guess," Shawn said, with a long look toward second. Second base was his usual spot.

"Heather?"

Heather looked up from the sidelines. She was holding her baby listlessly. "Me?"

"Yes, you," the coach said.

Her eyes brightened, then she frowned. "I don't have no glove."

"Plus she can't run because her tits bounce too much," Gina added.

Heather took an automatic slap at Gina, who ducked safely.

"No glove. Let's see," the coach said, stroking his chin. "I want Billy to pitch some. . . . So how about catcher? You can use my glove."

Heather shrugged, but a small grin came onto her face. Then she remembered her baby; she glanced back to Dale Schwartz, who sat in his car, smoking.

"*Bebé*," Mrs. González said, beckoning for the infant. "I hold *bebé*."

"I want first base," Gina called, but Mavis was already moving toward first base.

"Sorry. First is taken," she said.

"How about center field?" the coach said to Gina.

"With him out there?" Gina said, pointing to Danny Boyer. "No way!"

"Okay. Right field."

With a wary eye cast toward Danny, Gina scurried off to far right.

The coach looked around. "So we're missing only a center fielder. Mr. González?"

"No," Manuel said abruptly. "I must save my legs for the beet fields, for the beeg boss, Crystal Sugar."

The coach looked to Ole Svendson, who watched from his truck. Ole shrank slightly lower in the cab. "Guess not, huh?" the coach said with a glance to Mavis.

"You're getting to know the neighbors pretty well," Mavis said, laughing.

"I know who can play center field," Billy said. He put his fingers to his lips and whistled. Skinner came loping across the diamond. Billy trotted with him to center field. Once there, he knelt and spoke softly, earnestly to Skinner. The old dog wagged his tail madly but remained in place.

"There you have it!" the coach called. "Let's have some fielding."

At home plate the coach looked over his infield. "We're gonna do some basic defensive situations. No hard throws until everybody's warmed up, okay?"

They all nodded.

"Nobody out, play's at first." The coach batted

a soft bouncer to Shawn, who scooped and threw nicely to Mavis.

"Very nice. Same play, Jesús, okay?"

Jesús nodded impatiently.

The coach chopped a medium bouncer to Jesús, who played it expertly: range to the right; dip; scoop; throw. It was all done in fluid, wheeling motion, cat smooth and twice as quick.

The coach stared briefly at Jesús, then turned to his brother. "Raúl—same thing."

"*Sí.*"

The coach bounced one at Raúl, who gobbled up the ball, curving his body around it like a hawk scooping up a stray mouse, then made a sharp, sidearm flip to first. Billy glanced at the coach—who returned the look with a smile.

Then the coach turned his attention to Billy's mother. "Mrs. Baggs—the play's at home."

"It's *Mavis*," she said, fielding her grounder and throwing back to the plate.

The coach smiled. "Okay, Mavis! Good job, infield!" he called. He turned to the outfield.

"Danny, are you ready?"

Danny stood there.

The coach lofted a soft fly ball, which fell a few yards from the motionless Danny.

The Erickson girls groaned. The coach tried it again. Again the ball dropped beside Danny. Coach Anderson jogged out to left. Billy watched him out there talking with Danny, forming Danny's hands into a cup, dropping the ball over and over into his hands.

Mr. González fidgeted impatiently. After a while, Danny looked up at the sky, then down to the ball in his hands.

"Yes!" the coach said. "That's it." He came back and lofted another soft fly to Danny. This time, though Danny didn't stir from his spot, he actually held out his hands.

"Excelente!" Mrs. González called from her chair, with a glance toward her husband.

The coach tried a couple more flies with Danny, who seemed to watch the ball more each time. "You're catching on, Danny. Good job."

To Skinner, in center field, the coach bounced a base hit.

"Fetch!" Billy shouted.

Skinner broke from his spot and nabbed the ball on its first bounce, after which he raced wildly to the pitcher's mound, where Billy waited.

"Good dog," Billy said, and the spectators clapped.

"Center field looks solid." The coach laughed. "Next—Gina."

Gina had good reaction time, and her stubby legs propelled her under the fly ball, which she caught handily.

"Good!" Coach Anderson called.

And so they practiced. The sun sank unnoticed, lower and lower to the tree line, and the dew crept onto the grass. The coach called out imaginary situations—runner on first, no outs.

Runners on first and third, one out. Bases loaded, no outs. He patiently explained, mainly to his outfield, why the ball should go to a certain spot.

Jesús and Raúl fidgeted, tossed pebbles; they spoke occasionally in Spanish and snickered.

"Okay, Jesús—one out, runner on first, take two," the coach called to Jesús.

Jesús set himself.

The coach chopped a hard grounder to Jesús's left. It was clearly a base hit up the middle—but Jesús dove, gloved and shoveled the ball to second—where Raúl pirouetted on the bag like a ballet dancer for the relay throw to first.

Billy stared. Jesús had never touched the ball with his throwing hand; his quick scoop and shovel to Raúl—it was all leather. Billy had never seen that done before.

Coach Anderson smiled.

"Raúl—take two." The coach hit a sharp bouncer to Raúl's right. Raúl speared it, spun left and sidearmed the ball to second. There Jesús, in perfect timing, floated over second base, where he caught the ball, dipped a foot to graze the bag, then rifled the ball on to first.

"Wow!" Billy murmured.

Manuel's lips curled in satisfaction.

After Mavis finished her double play, the coach called a break. Dale Schwartz motored slowly away down the driveway (Gina gave him the middle finger) as Heather, holding her baby, stared after him. Mavis soon appeared with a great, sweating jar filled with grape Kool-Aid.

"And cookies, too—may miracles never cease," said the smiling, perspiring Coach Anderson.

"Milagros, sí," María said, "there are many miracles."

"Practice makes miracles," Manuel retorted.

María clucked her tongue apologetically and crossed herself.

As the group sat on the grass and munched their snack, Manuel spoke to his boys in Spanish, all the while making motions with his hands. Clearly he was talking baseball; his sons listened intently.

As their talk went on, Billy thought of major-league players with Spanish names.

Clemente.

Cardena.

Tovar.

Rodriquez.

Many more. He had never realized how many Spanish-speaking players there were. Baseball belonged not just to the United States, or to any country. Baseball belonged to everyone, and it belonged most to those who played it most.

When Manuel was finished, Billy turned to Jesús. "Where did you learn that one play, when you flip to second with only the glove?"

Jesús shrugged. "In Mexico we can play ball every day of the year."

"Lucky," Billy said. "Here in winter the snow is this high." He held his hand to the top of the Gonzálezes' car.

The eyes of María widened. *"Nieve? Monton de nieve? Ees impossible!"* she said.

"Snow that high, it's true," the coach said.

"No winter ball," Manuel said.

"Some winter ball," the coach ventured.

"Ees not possible—" Manuel replied.

"Show him, Billy," the coach said.

Billy found the orange baseball and tossed it to Manuel, who, for the first time, allowed a ghost of a smile on his face. He flipped the ball to Jesús, who grinned as well.

Billy drained his Kool-Aid. "Come on," Billy said to Jesús and Raúl as he grabbed his glove.

The González brothers hopped up immediately; their gloves, too, were never out of reach.

"I've had enough ball for tonight," Mavis said. She headed over to Ole Svendson's truck with a glass of Kool-Aid and a handful of cookies.

"Me, too," Heather said. She took back her baby from María González and actually held him close, like a real mother would.

And in the last half hour of light, the baseball continued. The Farm Team took batting practice.

Billy pitched.

He pitched underhanded to Big Danny, who, as might be expected, was taking all the way.

He pitched overhanded and slow to Gina and

Heather—who swung wildly though they managed a couple of raps.

Then it was the boys' turn.

"Okay—let's put some heat on it," the coach called to Billy. Jesús, Raúl and Shawn waited to bat. The coach pulled on his catcher's mask.

"Give me a couple of more warm-ups," Billy called to the coach.

Jesús remained out of the box. And Billy, from a full wind-up, arrowed one to the plate.

Manuel grunted his appreciation at Billy's speed.

Jesús glanced toward Raúl, who glanced toward his father—but he was occupied with watching Billy.

His next pitch was even faster, a smoker on the inside corner. Jesús, to the side, practiced his swing; it was a good way for the waiting batter to work on his timing.

"Batter up!" the coach called.

Jesús dug in. He took two more smooth, level practice swings, then readied himself. Billy let go a fastball.

Jesús, with a whip-quick swing, fouled the ball straight back, where it ricocheted off the corncrib, then lit squarely in the back of Ole Svendson's pickup and rattled about sharply. The hermit quickly got out and retrieved the ball, which he tossed with a surprisingly strong throw back to the plate.

"Sorry," Mavis called to him. "We should have a backstop."

Ole waved self-consciously. "No damage." He had a squeaky, rusty voice.

Since he was already out of his truck, Mavis waved him closer. "Come over and sit for a spell, Ole."

And *milagro* of *milagros*, he did.

Billy focused once again on the plate. He got Jesús on another foul, then tried to fool him with an off-speed pitch. Well back on his heels, never overcommitted, Jesús waited—then rapped a hard single to left.

"Good job—both of you," the coach called.

Billy got Raúl on three hard fastballs. He was not yet strong enough to catch up to Billy's smoke, but Raúl had a honey-sweet swing. He shrugged, smiling, as he handed the bat to Shawn.

Shawn managed a pop fly to center, which Gina caught in the deepening dusk.

"Getting pretty dark, folks," the coach said, standing and pulling off his mask.

"Jesús, again at the plate!" Manuel ordered.

The coach glanced over.

"It ees very good for my boys to see a real fastball," Manuel said.

"Quickly then," the coach called to Billy.

And Billy obliged. He threw fastballs for another five minutes until Jesús himself stepped out of the box and held up his hands. "Too dark, Papa."

"*Sí,*" Manuel said begrudgingly.

"We need lights," Billy called to his mother. "If we had lights, we could play all night."

She laughed. "I'd say that's plenty of baseball for one evening."

"I agree," the coach said. As he packed up his gear, he inquired (as Billy knew he would) about summer baseball—in Flint—for Jesús and Raúl.

"Ees not possible," Manuel said. "We must work in the sugar-beet fields during the day. That ees why night *beisbol* ees best for my boys."

"Will you come again here?" the coach said, gesturing to the farm baseball field.

"Ees a long drive from Crookston," María González began apologetically.

"We will come," Manuel said firmly. "For Billy's fastball, we will come." He nodded to Billy.

Billy grinned shyly and looked away.

"Good—we're happy to have you anytime," Mavis said. "In fact, I'm hoping you'll stay tonight."

"No—we leave tonight," Manuel said. Gloria and the boys turned to break camp, though they moved very slowly.

"Please. I insist you stay," Mavis said.

María looked hopefully at her husband, as did the children toward their father.

"Ees no trouble?" María said, adding, "We have all our own things."

"Plenty of room," Mavis said, gesturing to the dusky yard. "Tomorrow morning, early, I'll make pancakes, and then you can be off to Crookston."

Manuel and María González spoke briefly to each other in Spanish, during which he gestured once to the garden. María nodded, then turned to Mavis. "We will stay tonight. *Muchas gracias.*"

Before Billy fell asleep that night, he took one last look out his window. The outline of the diamond still showed faintly in the moonlight, and beside it was the González family encampment. A homemade tent covered the rear of their car. Juan Elvis, Gloria and Mrs. González slept inside the car, Manuel and the boys in hammocks stretched from the bumper to the door handles. In the darkness the hammocks hung alongside the car like black, curving cocoons. Billy drifted off to sleep seeing the brothers, Jesús and Raúl, suspended in the air, floating over second base as they turned yet another immaculate double play.

On Saturday it rained, which seemed right. Billy's mood was as low and gray as the clouds.

"They'll be back," Mavis said, meaning the González family.

"I doubt it," Billy said.

Mavis ignored his pessimism. "And that was so nice of them, hoeing the garden for us."

Billy didn't reply. It was one more thing to feel lousy about. He should have had the garden hoed long ago, and because he hadn't, the González family had done it for him. This morning during milking Billy had stepped to the open barn door for a breath of fresh air, and that's when he'd seen them: The whole family, little Juan Elvis in a sling on María's back, was moving steadily through the garden, their hoes rising and falling, flashing in the raw early-morning light.

"And the coach. It was kind of him to come. You'd think that man would be tired of baseball by the time Friday night rolls around."

"Not old Coach Anderson," Billy said, his spirits lifting slightly.

"The Farm Team looked good, don't you think?" Mavis said.

Billy knew she was just trying to cheer him, and he wouldn't fall for that old trick. Not on a dull, empty, rainy day on the farm. He shrugged. "What's the use of having a team if there's no one to play?"

"Last night was just the beginning," she said. "I'll bet we have more players next time, and more the time after that."

Billy stared glumly through the kitchen window off to the fields.

"The week will go fast," Mavis said. "Before you know it, Friday night will be here again."

But not soon enough, considering that Tuesday was looming. Tuesday was the day the social worker was coming.

The dreaded "home evaluation" visit.

This was Billy's leftover trouble from helping Abner crush the Randy Meyers A-1 Cars lot. For the most part Billy had managed to put the social worker out of his mind, but Tuesday she was arriving on the farm for real.

Her visit was not a matter of small concern for Mavis. By Monday night Billy's mother was worried to pacing. "There should be an adult around," Mavis fretted as she moved about the kitchen. "Your coach told me that that's what social workers like to see, an adult on the premises."

"I don't need no adult around," Billy said with disgust.

"Any adult—" Mavis said, correcting him. "And truthfully I'd feel better if there was an adult around this summer. Not that I don't trust you," she added.

Billy shrugged.

She paced beside the kitchen table. "I could stay home on Tuesday, but everybody knows I work full-time at Doctors' Clinic," she muttered.

"Maybe the coach could just happen to be here."

"I thought of that. But she wouldn't fall for that—she knows the coach, knows he lives in town. If only there was someone . . ."

They were silent for a spell. "I've got an idea," Billy said. "How about Big Danny?"

His mother stared. Despite the problem they were facing, she began to laugh.

"Big Danny's an adult," Billy retorted. "He's over twenty-one."

"Billy, he's—"

"So all the better. It's not like he'll be talking to her, will he?"

"But one look and she'd think—"

"One look close up, maybe. But what if it wasn't close up?"

Mavis thought about that.

"He could be . . . my uncle," Billy said. "My Uncle Dan."

Mavis's skeptical look began to return—until Billy said, "Robert would like it."

She looked up quickly at Billy.

"Really, it's Robert's kind of thing. He'd be

highly proud of us," Billy said, grinning at his mother.

"Okay, okay," she said, "we'll give it a try." A faint gleam of a smile grew in her own eyes.

On Tuesday morning Mavis fetched Big Danny, who took his usual spot in the rear of the pickup. She was not happy at all about this, but right now it was the best plan they had.

"Your shoes? Where are your shoes?" Mavis said suddenly to Danny; his huge bare feet and filthy toes rested on the bumper.

Danny, of course, had no comment.

Mavis headed to the Boyer house, if you could call it that, a tumbledown tar-paper affair. From the porch she called out, "Do you know where Danny's shoes are?"

A voice rasped through the screen door. "He don't want to wear shoes, he don't have to wear shoes." It was Danny's father, Byron Boyer, an alcoholic farmer who kept a few hogs and drew a disability pension from the Korean War. "You want him to work for you, you take him as is. That's what I had to do, din't I?"

Mavis sighed and returned to the truck. She drove off liking this plan less every minute.

At home, Billy greeted Danny in his usual way. "Hey, Danny, what say?"

"You know, Billy, I wish you wouldn't say that every time," Mavis said.

"Say what?"

"You know very well what," Mavis muttered.

"Now shake a leg. We've got work to do."

They got Danny dressed in clean farm coveralls and a new cap and pair of rubber boots. Danny did not seem happy about any of it, particularly the blue coveralls, which were tight on him; he kept tugging at the buttons, at the sleeves, at the crotch.

"It's okay, Danny," Billy said. "Once the old-crow social worker has come and gone, you can take everything off."

Danny frowned and looked off down the road and tugged again at his crotch.

"This is not going to work," Mavis said, her voice rising. She checked her watch. "She's due any minute."

"Sure it's going to work," Billy said. "Come on, Uncle Dan."

Big Danny blinked several times at his new name, then followed Billy toward the barn. He took large careful steps in the rubber boots, as if testing their weight.

"We're going to be cleaning the gutter when she arrives, Uncle Dan. Even a social worker wouldn't come in the barn when there's shit being pitched."

Inside the barn, stooping low—for his cap nearly brushed the ceiling joists—Danny took up the shovel and looked for the wheelbarrow. Danny was at home in a barn.

Outside, right on time, Billy heard tires scrape on gravel.

"I'll be back in a little while," Billy said. "Keep going on the gutter." He had started Danny at the far end of the barn, to keep him distant from the front door.

Danny fidgeted in his tight coveralls, tugged at the sleeves, at the crotch.

Outside, Billy saw his mother speaking with the social worker, Mrs. Sanders. Mavis was chatting and smiling like this was a Walt Disney movie. Mrs. Sanders kept glancing about the farm. Which of course Billy and Mavis had made sure was extra tidy. The lawn was mowed. The screen door was patched and oiled at the hinges. A pot of fresh-looking petunias smiled from the front step.

"Is that an outhouse?" Mrs. Sanders asked, looking across the yard at the edge of the windbreak. She seemed prepared to write something on her clipboard.

"Used to be, yes," Mavis said. "Of course we have indoor plumbing now. Have had for some time."

"How long?" Mrs. Sanders asked. She was eyeballing the worn path to the old biffy's door.

"Gosh, it's hard to remember, it's been so long," Mavis drawled, pretending to look at Billy for help. "At least ten years, maybe more?"

Billy's eyes widened. He remembered using the outdoor biffy, remembered its cold seat on his butt in winter, its spiders and hornets' nest in summer. He still used it once in a while when he was too muddy or manure-splashed to go into the house, and Abner used it regularly. Abner still was not at home with indoor plumbing; he thought all cesspools would eventually fill up and quit working. But the fact was that the Baggs family had gotten an indoor toilet only three years ago.

"We only keep the old outhouse around in case our cesspool should freeze up in winter," Mavis said easily. "One needs a backup system, wouldn't you agree?"

"Yes, I suppose you're right," Mrs. Sanders said. She turned to Billy. "Hello there, young man," she said, fixing a smile on her face. Her eyes ran up and down him just like they moved up and down the old outhouse.

Billy had on clean clothes. "Good morning," he said in a cheerful voice. "Nice to see you again, ma'am."

Mavis's eyes widened.

The social worker's eyes narrowed.

"Here, Skinner," Billy called, and began to toss the old ball around.

"One nice thing about living in the country," Mavis said quickly, "is that a boy can have his dog."

"Yes, that's true," Mrs. Sanders allowed.

Billy romped with Skinner.

"Come on in," Mavis said, as if Mrs. Sanders were a long-lost sister. Over the woman's shoulder Mavis glared at Billy and motioned for him to cut the overacting.

Billy grinned. After the door slammed, he hung around close enough to eavesdrop. Mavis chattered on, and the voices moved room to room.

"You've actually quite a tidy, serviceable house here," the social worker said.

"Why, thank you."

His mother's voice brought to mind a velvet mitten covering a balled-up fist. Billy figured Mavis could hold it together about another five minutes before she knocked Mrs. Sanders right through the screen door and clear to Kingdom Come.

"Mother," Billy called, "may I go to the barn and see Uncle Dan?"

There was silence. Then Mavis replied, in her best cheery voice, "In a little while, dear."

"Uncle Dan?" Mrs. Sanders inquired.

"My brother," Mavis said to the social worker. "My brother. Younger brother. He's here this summer. Well, you know, what with Abner away and with me working, well, we needed some-one—an adult—around."

"Yes, of course," Mrs. Sanders said.

Billy imagined he heard her pencil scraping and scribbling on the page.

"Well, I've actually got to run off to work," Mavis said. "Billy can answer any further questions you have. And of course Uncle Dan is in the barn."

On her way out Mavis showed Billy a glare

and a real balled-up fist, both directed backward to the social worker—who did not realize, Billy was certain, how close she'd come to getting a hard left hook to the kisser.

"'Bye, son," Mavis called sweetly to Billy, and drove off.

The pickup left, and though Mavis spun the tires briefly, all in all it was a hell of a performance.

"Staying out of trouble these days?" said Mrs. Sanders, patting him on the shoulder.

"Yes, ma'am," Billy said. He did not feel quite so much like acting, now that he was alone with this pale person with strong perfume. But he endured her presence, showing her about the farm—the chickens, the calves frisking in the little pasture—and answering her questions— which went on and on—as best he could. He lied about nearly everything but did so with an earnest look and occasionally even a smile. Finally she said, "Your Uncle Dan—may I meet him?"

"Sure," Billy said. He pointed toward the barn.

As they headed across the yard, Billy stayed two steps upwind of the woman; her dime-store rosewater perfume made him gag. Nearing the barn door, they heard the scrape of the manure scoop. Mrs. Sanders's nose began to wrinkle up when she was still several paces away.

"He's cleaning the gutter," Billy said.

Mrs. Sanders slowed. "Perhaps I'll just peek in and wave hello."

"Fine," Billy said.

Mrs. Sanders arrived beside him and peered into the dim barn.

Hearing voices, the towering blond bulk of Big Danny Boyer appeared just a few steps inside. He had removed the tight, itchy coveralls. He had removed the uncomfortable, strange cap. And while he was at it, he had removed his underwear. Everything was off except his rubber boots. He stood there holding his manure fork, staring at Mrs. Sanders.

Mrs. Sanders froze. The only thing moving were her eyes, which dropped to Danny's midsection. Her jaw slacked.

Billy could certainly see why they called him Big Danny.

A croaking noise came from Mrs. Sanders, who began to back away from the door in clumsy steps, her eyes still on Danny's lower parts.

Big Danny, curious, followed to the doorway.

Turning, Mrs. Sanders half ran, half waddled to her car.

Danny stepped outside into full daylight. He held up his shovel—his way of waving—as the sedan raced off down the driveway.

Billy sighed. "Oh well, Uncle Dan," he said, "we tried."

CHAPTER

21

And then there was the unfinished business of the dimes.

Six thousand dollars' worth of dimes.

On Wednesday morning a woman from the First Farmers' Bank called to tell Billy the dimes had finally arrived from the treasury in Saint Paul.

"When will you be picking them up?" she asked.

"This afternoon right after lunch," Billy said. One of his personal lessons, something he had learned on his own this summer, was this: Do the worst first. Do what was troublesome and pesky right away; otherwise it nagged and nagged like a pebble in his boot or a wood tick crawling somewhere inside his shirt. Billy could smell trouble with Abner's plan to repay Randy Meyers, and that being the case, he might as well get it over with.

At the jail Abner was lying on his cot reading an actual book. Billy jerked to a halt and stared; he could feel air on his teeth. He had never seen Abner reading a book. But sure enough, his father held a thin, shiny book and was moving his lips.

"Hi, Pa."

All in one motion Abner stashed the book under his pillow and sat up. "What the hell! You sure know how to sneak up on a guy."

"Sorry, Pa."

There were some other things on his cot: a tape recorder and some brochures, all of which Abner set about putting away. "Wait there. Give me a minute to get organized."

Billy waited. "So what were you reading?"

"Nothing."

Billy glanced down. The thin, golden spine of the book showed: *Sinbad the Sailor*. Also one of the cassette tapes lay uncovered, its title *Phonics for Easy Reading*.

"Too much damn junk in here," Abner muttered, sweeping all the reading material into a box. "The coach brings this stuff. It all belongs to him. We play cards a couple times a week, and he always ends up leaving his school things behind."

Billy nodded.

"How a guy that forgetful can be a teacher is beyond me," Abner said.

Billy looked down, and after a short silent stretch, they began their usual talk.

"So, anything new at home?"

"Nope, not a thing," Billy said, glancing off through the window.

"Any strangers coming around? Anything I should know about?"

"No," Billy said quickly. Before Abner could

press further, Billy handed him the weekly slip from the milk-truck driver. "Thought you might want to take a look at the this."

Abner examined the receipt; he let out a low whistle. "All together the herd is up over a hundred pounds of milk a day." He looked at Billy. Billy shrugged.

"You doing something different?" his father said, raising an eyebrow.

"Not really. Well, maybe some little things here and there," Billy said casually.

"It must be the pasture. The grass must be extra good this summer."

"That's probably it," Billy muttered. Someday he would tell Abner about the soybean meal, but today did not feel like the right time.

Abner did some figuring on the milk poundage. "That's close to three hundred dollars a month, extra. Hell—I ought to go to jail more often."

Billy didn't laugh. He stared straight at Abner. "It ain't no fun having you in jail, Pa."

Abner looked away, at the floor. "I agree," he said at length. He gazed about the cell. "Truth is I can't wait to get out of this bird cage. Get home to some peace and quiet. Get clear the hell away from people. The sheriff says if I pay Meyers promptly, he'll speak to the judge about letting me work at home during the week." He looked at Billy.

"I got the dimes," Billy said. He was hoping that Abner might change his plan, that he would just hand over the money without any fuss.

But a slow, narrow-lipped grin grew on Abner's face. "All six thousand dollars' worth?"

Billy nodded.

"Harvey," Abner called out to the front office.

"The sheriff's busy," the woman jailor called back.

"Get him unbusy. Tell him I'm all ready to pay that crook Meyers and get square with the law," Abner said.

There was a long sigh and some clattering about. Presently the sheriff himself appeared.

"You're gonna pay Meyers?" he said suspiciously.

"Yup, I am," Abner said. "Billy here is going to the bank to get the money, and he's gonna deliver it to Meyers himself."

"Cash?" Harvey said.

"Yup, all six thousand."

"That's a lot a money for a kid to be totin' around," the sheriff answered.

"Exactly what I was thinking," Abner said. "Maybe you or a deputy could go along and make sure nothing happens? Be sort of a witness?"

"I suppose," Harvey said, checking his watch. "I'll have somebody at the bank in a little while."

"And give Meyers a call, too," Abner said. "Make sure he's there to get his money."

"He'll be there," the sheriff said. "You can bet on that."

At the First Farmers' Bank Billy brought the

pickup around to the front door. Sheriff Olson himself stood inside the bank, chatting with the ladies.

Billy went to the window and signed for the dimes.

"They're rather heavy," the clerk said. "Several bags of them."

"I've got a truck," Billy said.

Sheriff Olson turned and began to pay more attention.

"This way please."

The sheriff followed Billy back into the vault. There, on two hand trucks, were stacks and stacks of bags, heavy canvas bags, of dimes. Each was zipped shut and sealed with a blob of red sealing wax. The sheriff hefted one of the bags; it jingled.

"Holy smokes," the sheriff said, turning to Billy. "You're not . . ."

"Six thousand dollars is six thousand dollars," Billy said.

"It's all here," the clerk said apologetically to the sheriff.

The sheriff let drop the bag, took off his hat and let out a sigh. "I ought to retire," he said. "The wife and I have got a cabin out on Little Turtle Lake. We could live there full-time and have no problems of any kind."

Billy waited for the sheriff to say more.

"Go ahead," he said abruptly to Billy. "If it was anybody but Abner Baggs behind this, I'd figure out some way to stop you, but that would only prolong things. So just get it over with."

Outside the bank, Billy loaded the bags one by one in the pickup bed. The weight of the load began to settle the rear springs; Billy guessed there must be close to five hundred pounds' worth. When they were all loaded, Billy hopped up onto the pile of coin bags and broke a wax seal. He unzipped the bag and dumped it. The coins showered out water bright and as loud as breaking glass.

Waiting in his car, the sheriff only shook his head.

Within a few minutes Billy had emptied all the bags and returned them to the staring bank clerk. "I won't be needing these," Billy said.

At Randy Meyers A-1 Cars, Randy Meyers waited in a late-model Cadillac. He was smoking a short cigar and smiling. Billy drove up in the pickup with the sheriff behind.

"Got your money," Billy said.

"'Bout time, kid," Meyers said, getting out of his car. He had put on weight since Billy last saw him, and his hair was rounded up beauty-shop tight around his ears like he was a Las Vegas singer.

"Crime doesn't pay, kid, that's the lesson here, right, Sheriff?"

The sheriff had no response.

"So where is it?" Meyers said, approaching the truck.

Billy got out and pointed into the rear. "Right here."

Meyers came around back and his eyes bugged out. "Dimes?"

"Yup. Sixty thousand of them."

Color rose in Meyers's neck and cheeks. "Are you nuts? Are you insane? Of course you are—this is the Baggs family I'm dealing with."

"Yup, it is," Billy said politely. He jerked open the end gate, and several pounds of silver poured down over the bumper.

"My money!" Meyers shouted.

"It's all here," Billy said. As Meyers knelt to gather up the spilled dimes, Billy got into the truck and brought up the rpms. With a jerk he dropped the clutch pedal—and dimes flooded out the rear, nearly covering Randy Meyers. Billy steered the truck in a roaring tight circle, which slung the dimes into a silvery halo onto the blackened, cindery car lot.

"There's some kind of law being broken here, Sheriff!" Meyers shouted, standing in the circle with his fist upraised at Billy.

"I thought so, too," the sheriff said, "but for the life of me I can't think what it would be."

"What am I supposed to do now?!" Meyers wailed.

"Sell better cars next time?" the sheriff said. With that he drove off. Billy was already long gone down the highway, headed home.

CHAPTER

22

With the tractor and mower Billy cut hay all day Friday, twenty acres of it. By late afternoon the scent of clover and alfalfa hung over the Baggs farm like perfume, and it was into that sweet fragrance that bicycles, motorbikes, and cars began to arrive for Friday-night baseball.

Ole Svendson parked alongside the ball field before Billy had finished milking.

Heather and Gina Erickson came in time for supper. Billy's mother glanced at the clock with an irritated look but went ahead and set out two more plates. "Gina—make some use of yourself and shell that pan of peas. Heather, you've got time to give that baby a bath in the summer sink while things are cooking," Mavis instructed. "And don't spare the soap."

"Is Dale Schwartz coming again tonight?" Heather asked. She held her baby more natural-like these days; she seemed to stand up straighter, and had lost a few pounds, too.

"I'm not sure—why?" Mavis asked.

Heather wouldn't answer.

Byron Boyer arrived in an old truck with a six-pack of beer in the front and Big Danny in the rear. "Well, I'll be," Mavis exclaimed, looking out the window. "That's the first time I've seen that man take his son anywhere when it wasn't for work." Danny got out of the rear with no prodding from anyone and went straightaway to left field, where he stood in exactly the same spot as last week.

Shawn Howenstein arrived in a cloud of dust on his buzzing motor scooter.

The McGintys, a sheep-raising family from the rocky north end of the township, arrived in their pickup; two shaggy-haired boys who rode Billy's school bus leaped from the rear and bounded onto the field.

The coach drove in promptly at six o'clock and shook hands with everyone, after which he rounded up the Farm Team for stretching and general loosening-up activities.

As he did toe-touches, Billy kept looking down the road for the González family, for their old station wagon with gear and luggage piled on top. Twice he saw a newer, shinier station wagon drive by, a car he did not recognize. But no González family.

When Billy looked up again, the shiny station wagon was coming up the driveway. Billy squinted. Strangers. Probably lost tourists. The car eased to a stop, and the driver got out and peered about. He was a pale, skinny man wearing a new golf shirt, walking shorts several sizes too big for his skinny white legs, and black socks with sandals. In the rear of the car, his head out the window, a boy surveyed the farm, the diamond and the team.

"Hello there," Mavis called out.

"Good evening," the man said cautiously. He had curly dark hair and thick glasses. His kid had the same dark hair and glasses. The wife stayed put in the car; she did not appear pleased to be here. "I'm Jacob Goldberg. From Minneapolis?"

"What can we do for you?" Mavis said.

"Ah . . . well," the man began, stammering slightly, "my wife and son and I are here on vacation at the lake, at Hilda's Resort—"

"Which is the pits, the absolute pits," his wife added.

The man laughed shrilly. "My wife, Rita."

The farm crowd stared.

"She's right, of course. Hilda's Resort doesn't have much for recreation," Mr. Goldberg said. "I mean, really nothing for my son, Aaron. Shuffleboard is about all there is at Hilda's." He laughed his high-pitched laugh again.

"Shuffleboard and paddleboat," Rita Goldberg remarked with sarcasm.

"Well, you said you wanted someplace quiet," her husband said.

"Quiet, yes. Dead, no," Rita Goldberg said, getting out, looking around. "Where I work, complete silence is not a good sign."

Ignoring his parents, the narrow-shouldered boy kept staring at the Farm Team. His unblinking eyes traveled across Billy and the others one by one. It was not an unfriendly stare. It was not a shy stare. It was more a mathematical kind of look.

"When we were in town today, exploring, we ventured into the Feedmill," Mr. Goldberg said. "I've always thought it important for a city kid—especially a studious boy like Aaron—to get out and see the countryside, the small towns."

"So we went to the Flint Feedmill," Rita Goldberg continued. "Can you believe it? Some families go to Yellowstone Park, some go to Florida, but no—we end up at the Flint Feedmill."

"I rather liked the Feedmill," the boy, Aaron, said evenly.

"Good for you," Mavis said. "That's what vacations are for, I should think—to do different things."

"Anyway, to make a long story short," Mr. Goldberg said, "at the Feedmill we saw the flier, about baseball at the Baggs farm? 'Come one, come all'?"

"You're at the right place," Mavis said. "Welcome."

Mr. Goldberg looked relieved. "Here we are, Aaron," he called.

"I can see the diamond, Father, I'm not blind." Aaron adjusted his glasses on the bridge of his nose and stepped out of the car. He was not much larger than Tiny Tim Loren, and he carried a stiff-looking baseball glove that looked as long as his arm.

"There aren't any snakes around, are there?" Mr. Goldberg asked suddenly.

"Father, the only poisonous snakes in Minnesota live on the rocky bluffs along the Minnesota River," Aaron said evenly, "which is three hundred miles south-southwest from here." He continued to survey the team, the field.

"My son, the egghead," Mr. Goldberg said, shrugging. "Takes after his mother." He laughed briefly.

"Come on, Aaron," Mavis said, "let me introduce you to everyone."

Aaron made the rounds, stepping forward to shake hands with one and all, including Big Danny Boyer, with the same short pumping motion and the same steady gaze. The simple act of a handshake with a stranger was too much for the country kids; their personalities collapsed, one by one, into fits of giggling or stupidity. Gina Erickson stuck her hands in her armpits and said, "How old *are* you, anyway?" (To Billy the new kid did seem like he was way too old for his skinny body.)

"Fifteen, just," Aaron said pleasantly as he continued his round of hand shaking.

"Kids don't shake hands," Gina said, stepping back. "You're weird."

"Ninth grade? Do you play ball, then, in

Minneapolis, Aaron?" Coach Anderson inquired as Mavis hustled Gina off for a talk about manners.

"Well he *is* weird," Gina whispered as Mavis hoisted her along by one arm and one ear.

"I don't care if someone is from outer space—there's such a thing as manners," Mavis hissed as they disappeared behind the corncrib.

Out of sight, Gina cried, "Ow!"

"Me? Play ball? In a manner of speaking, yes," Aaron said, turning his attention once again to the coach and the field.

"What school?"

"Highland Academy," Aaron said. "I'm a lousy player. What I enjoy most is managing, strategizing."

The coach smiled. "Up here our main strategy is to catch the ball, hit the ball. As you see, it's an informal team."

"Refreshingly so," Aaron said, surveying the farm kids once more. "Sometimes in the city leagues a team's chemistry is lost because of an overly rigid framework of rules and expectations."

Billy and Shawn Howenstein looked at each other.

"'Refreshingly so'?" Shawn whispered.

"'Team chemistry'?" Billy murmured.

Aaron went on to explain in a clear, direct manner how the aspect of having fun provides a kind of glue that holds the best teams tightly together.

"You gotta have fun, no doubt about it," the coach said. Beneath his big arm he swept Aaron Goldberg forward onto the field. "So let's have some." The overly serious kid from Minneapolis smiled for the first time.

But he wasn't kidding when he said he was a lousy player.

The first ball tossed to Aaron hit his thumb.

The second ball dropped from his glove like a brick.

When he threw, he was clumsier still. His arm motion looked like a goose flopping a broken wing. He was a worse ballplayer than Tiny Tim Loren; Aaron Goldberg made Tiny Tim look like Pete Rose. In the middle of all this, a horn tooted and dust rolled up the driveway. It was the González station wagon.

"*Hola!*" Billy called, and waved like a fool— then recovered himself and tried to act a bit more cool.

Before the old station wagon had stopped, Jesús and Raúl were flying out its doors, racing with their gloves toward the field.

Billy skipped a ground ball to Jesús, who scooped on the short hop and flipped to Raúl, who went behind the back for the toss back to Billy.

"Welcome back, folks," the coach called to the González family. Mavis returned with Gina, who was red-faced and scowling, and propelled her onto the ball field.

"*Hola,*" Mavis said to María González, who smiled widely. Skinner's greeting was the usual, a thorough face licking for little Juan Elvis.

"Looks as if we've got plenty of players tonight," the coach said.

Around the yard were over a dozen vehicles, mostly battered farm pickups and older dusty sedans. Someone turned on a car radio, and country music began to twang soft and easy, echoing off the barn and about the field. Gradually a few more cars came, and even a couple of tractors. On a farm a crowd like this usually meant an auction, or bad news of some kind— but not here, not tonight. Even the arrival of Dale Schwartz could not dampen the mood. "I knew he'd come," Heather said, and fired the ball down to second base.

María González and Gloria set up a sturdy wooden table with some pots and food on it, as Mr. González erected the charcoal grill.

Mavis ran an electrical cord from the barn and brought out a large coffee percolator. And as the Farm Team played catch and raced about, soon enough there was coffee bubbling, and smoke rising from the grill, and hot oil spattering in the Gonzálezes' wide fry pan.

"You have not had your supper," Mavis observed.

"*Sí, sí,* we have. Tonight we make some real Mexican food, *tamales*, for the ballplayers and family."

On and off the field, people mingled and talked. Mrs. Goldberg cornered Ole Svendson and began to bend his ear about Hilda's Resort, about its lumpy beds, about its screens that let in mosquitoes, about the unraked beach. In shock, having never seen such a talkative woman, Ole nodded dumbly; his cheeks were scarlet. All along the fence the hum and buzz, the laughter and talk, went on.

"Ma—you playing first again tonight?" Billy called.

"Only if you need me."

"Okay," Billy said, slightly relieved. Though Mavis was a good-enough first basewoman, it was a little embarrassing playing on a team with his own mother.

So Billy claimed first base. Shawn took third, and Jesús and Raúl took their positions at second base and shortstop. The McGinty boys and the others filled in where needed.

Aaron Goldberg chose a clipboard; it looked natural in his hands. He stood close along the sideline and took detailed notes as the coach rapped fungoes to the infield.

"Take it to first, Shawn."

"Nice pivot, Jesús."

"Way to scoop, Raúl."

"Go to third, Billy—way to smoke it."

Aaron kept making notes as the coach turned to the outfield. The McGinty boys, Skinner and Gina hauled down fly balls like their gloves were magnets and the ball was a round steel bearing. Even Big Danny's head moved as he tracked the balls, and once or twice he went so far as to point with some precision to where they would land.

"Good job, Danny!" the coach called.

Aaron Goldberg recorded everything with equal consideration.

During a break in the infield practice Aaron Goldberg trotted out to see Billy. "I have some questions," he said.

Billy glanced at Shawn, who smirked.

"First, the mound seems to be a nonstandard distance from the plate."

Billy explained about splitting the distance between youth league and big league.

"A reasonable decision," Aaron said, "especially considering the variety in age and skill level here."

Billy watched him cross that off his list. He winked at Shawn, who snickered.

Aaron continued. "Second, I notice that the fans are not protected from foul balls. There is strong potential here for injury and/or lawsuit."

Billy looked toward home plate. The parents and spectators were busy talking and cooking and eating, paying no attention to the ball; some little kids, including Juan Elvis, played in the backs of pickups at eye level just a few yards behind the plate. A hard foul ball could indeed bean someone in the worst way.

"I doubt anybody here would sue us—at least

none of the locals," Billy said.

Aaron Goldberg kept his steady gaze.

"But yeah, you're right," Billy had to admit.

"For protection I suggest a verbal announcement this time," Aaron said, "and perhaps try to get some kind of inexpensive screen in place before next Friday night."

Billy squinted at the kid; Aaron Goldberg walked a very narrow line between making complete sense and pissing Billy off.

"The kind of wire mesh around your chicken barn would do just fine," Aaron added, pointing across the farmyard. "A couple of poles from your lumber pile and a few yards of wire would be sufficient."

"So who's going to put this up by next Friday?"

"I could come by and help."

Billy stared, then shrugged. "All right. If you want work, I'll give you some."

"And third question," Aaron continued, "the left fielder? Danny?"

"What about him?"

"He seems to be a slightly weak link out there," Aaron said with a faint note of apology in his voice.

"He's not weak, he's artistic."

"Artistic?" Aaron inquired.

"You know, silent. He has never said a word in his life."

"Autistic, you mean," Aaron replied.

"Whatever, but . . . but he's our left fielder," Billy added, firmly. "My ma says."

"Okay, okay," Aaron said easily, jotting something on his clipboard. "Most teams have their injured veteran, their sentimental favorite. We can work around Danny." He glanced down his list. "One last matter. We need a catcher."

"True," Billy admitted, lowering his voice so that Heather wouldn't overhear. Heather could throw well enough, but was afraid of catching Billy's fastball; in truth Billy worried about that too, about hitting her in the chest or something embarrassing like that. On the other hand, he didn't want to bench her, not right now. Playing ball was good for her. "But we've got to keep Heather behind the plate." He explained, briefly, about Heather and her baby.

"I see," Aaron said. "Okay." His eyes went slightly blank as his mind set to work on the problem—and in an instant he had a plan. He explained it to Billy, who scratched his head in amazement: This kid had two brains, maybe three.

Billy went over to the hay shed and came back with a bale of hay, the standard rectangular kind, which was about four feet by two by two. By thumping one end sharply a couple of times on the ground, Billy was able to make the bale stand upright behind home plate.

"All right!" Heather said; immediately she crouched behind the bale.

Aaron smiled. "Give it a try," he called to Billy and Heather.

Billy took the mound and rocketed in a fastball—which went *ploomp!* into the hay bale, then dropped harmlessly to the side, where Heather snatched it and tossed it back to Billy.

"Now we're cooking!" the coach called.

After a Kool-Aid and cookie break, the Farm Team took the field for some serious batting and strategizing. Aaron Goldberg several times stepped forward and murmured something to Coach Anderson, who listened to the kid with endless patience.

On the mound, Billy was able to bring his fastball up to speed, plus work on an off-speed pitch, a palm ball, that the coach had shown him. Palming the ball allowed him to keep the same pitching-arm motion but reduce the ball's speed by half, it seemed.

"Actually fifteen percent or less," Aaron interjected. "If a major leaguer's fastball is, say, ninety miles per hour, his change-up is eighty, eighty-two. But that, and the illusion of a greater reduction in speed, is often just enough to fool the batter."

"There you have it," the coach said, with a wink to Billy.

Aaron had his stopwatch and had been timing Billy's fastballs.

"So how fast is Billy's fastball?" Gina called, in her bet-you-can't-figure-that-one-out voice.

Aaron consulted his clipboard. "It's approximately—"

"Not important!" the coach shouted. "Let's stop worrying—all of you—about the numbers, and just play ball out here!"

So they did.

For at least two hours. On the sidelines the adults ate food and drank coffee and smoked cigarettes and talked and watched the baseballs fly and the sun sink toward the west. The cows finally drifted off to pasture as a new moon began to rise. And even Mr. González seemed satisfied with the workout.

In the last half hour of daylight, the coach bagged the hardball. "Enough!" he said. Then he tossed a softball hand to hand and smiled at the lazy adults. "Aaron. Make up two rosters. Let's get these parents off their duffs and have some good old-fashioned country kittenball to finish up the night."

"Great idea," Mavis called, and began to herd all the adults—even Ole Svendson and the Goldbergs—onto the field. Dale Schwartz, of course, was too cool to play, and drove off in his dusty yellow El Camino; and Gina, of course, gave him the middle finger.

To make things fair, everyone had to play softball barehanded. And as the dew came onto the field and purple light fell, they laughed and batted and chased the big white ball. Their game continued until dark was upon them and the softball floated through the air as uncatchable as the moon.

"Enough!" Mavis.

There were complaints from the kids but groans of relief from the adults. All the players headed, sweaty and glowing, toward the sidelines and the remainder of the food. They gathered around the Gonzálezes' grill, the smoke from which kept away the mosquitoes, and the kids began to roast marshmallows over the coals.

"You know, Coach," Billy said, rotating his swelling marshmallow, "our baseball team ain't all that bad."

The coach did not correct Billy's grammar. Not tonight. Lounging in the grass with the sweet scent of mowed hay and the woody smell of cattle and the tasty aroma of Mexican food and good old Midwestern coffee, he only leaned back and smiled and lit a little cigar.

"I, too, think it's a rather promising team," Aaron Goldberg added.

The coach gazed into the orange light of the grill.

"Heck, I'll bet we could beat the town team," Billy said.

The coach, puffing on his cigar, looked up. "Say again?"

Grinning, his protruding top teeth shiny in the firelight, Billy repeated himself.

"Beat my town team?" the coach said.

"Yes," Billy replied.

The coach scanned the players. "This bunch of marshmallow eaters beat my town team?"

The Farm Team nodded as one. "Yeah—yes—sure we could!"

"No way on God's green earth!" the coach retorted.

The country kids laughed and pitched a marshmallow or two at the coach.

When things had quieted down, Aaron Goldberg said, "There is, of course, only one true method of finding out."

The coach looked at Aaron Goldberg, then back at the rest of the expectant, eager country kids. "And just what would that 'method' be?"

"A game!" they said in one voice.

I n the new week, with hay down and the weather holding hot and dry, Billy hardly had time to think about baseball. But whenever he did, a smile came onto his face. The coach had agreed to a match-up between the Town Team and the Farm Team. It would be the biggest thing to happen on the Baggs farm since—

Since the death of his brother, Robert.

But Robert would be there at the game somehow, Billy knew, and at that thought Billy's mood lightened again as quickly as the sun emerging from behind a wind-blown cloud.

Monday morning, however, a shiny yellow vehicle turned Billy's mood dark. It was Dale Schwartz. His wavy, dark hair slicked back and gleaming, he got out and leaned against his El Camino. "Your old man asked me to come over and help with haying," Dale said, rolling a toothpick in his mouth.

"Got plenty of help," Billy said.

"Who? You and them wild Erickson girls?"

"Leave them out of this."

"Out of what?" Dale said.

"You know what."

"Kids nowadays," Dale said, "they watch too much TV or something. They got such wild imaginations."

"Heather's baby ain't imaginary."

"Dry up with that stuff," Dale said, quick as a snake. "I warned you about that kind of loose talk, and I'm warning you again right now."

Billy stood his ground. "I ain't taking any more shit from you, especially not here. I run this farm."

Dale looked around. "Oh, you run this farm, do you?" he said, faking a long yawn. "Well, your old man specifically asked me to help out with haying. Said it would be good to have an adult around."

"Not your kind of adult—"

Dale made a move to grab Billy, but Billy was quicker: In an instant he had Schwartz spun around and gripped in a half-nelson with one arm wrenched high up his back. He could smell Vitalis hair oil. "Get out of here, you creep!" he shouted, and ran Schwartz headfirst into his car through the window.

Slowly, shaking his head to clear it, Schwartz sat up in the driver's seat. He checked the mirror and smoothed his hair. He found another toothpick. "Okay, suit yourself, Billy-boy," he said, turning to squint at him. He was grinning again.

"But I'll be back. There's a big game Friday night, right? Neighbors always welcome, come one, come all, right?"

For the hay crew, Billy hired Byron Boyer, Danny's father, who was drinking less than usual these days; he could drive a tractor. Billy himself headed up the wagon-and-hayloft crew, which included Big Danny and Aaron Goldberg. The geeky city kid had arrived on the farm Monday morning (his father protesting the dangers of insects and falling objects) all set to work on the baseball field.

"You might be on vacation, but I ain't," Billy said crabbily to Aaron. "First I've got to put up hay today and most of this week. If you'd clean your glasses, you could see that." Billy pointed to the twenty-acre field striped with dry, fluffy, green windrows.

Aaron squinted across the farm. "So I'll help you put up the hay."

Billy looked down at Goldberg, at his chicken neck, his narrow shoulders, his scrawny arms. "Naw, probably not."

"It would be a worthwhile experience."

"It ain't an 'experience,' it's work. Hay bales are heavy."

"I'd like to try."

Billy chose another tack. "You could get hurt around the equipment. Get wrapped up in the power takeoff and lose an arm. Lose a leg. Lose your pecker."

Aaron blinked. "If anything, I'm a careful person."

Billy stared. There was no getting rid of this kid. "All right," he sighed, "suit yourself."

As the workday began, the sight of skinny Aaron Goldberg lugging bales alongside Big Danny Boyer at least was worth a laugh. Byron Boyer, the tractor driver, must have been thinking the same thing.

"If you two boys could horse-trade some of your brains and beef, you'd both be about normal," he called back to them.

Danny and Aaron looked at each other; both appeared to consider the idea.

And the tractor rolled on.

During the first round about the field, Billy kept a close eye on Aaron. As the first bales came up onto the wagon, Aaron, unlike most kids, did not show off his strength, did not clown around. He had good balance on the moving wagon, and what was more, he was efficient. By stacking two bales under the mouth of the baler chute, Aaron devised a clever, flipping motion that allowed him to bounce the rectangles of hay back to Danny by using the natural momentum and weight of each bale. "Why didn't I think of that?" Billy muttered to Skinner. For years Billy had been lugging the full weight of each bale to the rear of the wagon, then lifting it again onto the stack.

Still, by midafternoon Aaron was fading. He

could barely tip each bale. Most fell flat onto the boards, where he was forced to drag them backward across the wagon floor. Still, he managed to keep the bales moving. Aaron Goldberg was not a quitter. Once he stumbled and went down. Billy was about to signal a halt, but Aaron popped back up like a boxer pretending he had slipped; he shook his head to clear it, then groggily reached for the next bale. At this point in the day Billy had seen more than one farm kid throw in the towel and sit down—but Aaron Goldberg, dusty and red-faced and bent over, was still on his feet.

"Take a break," Billy called. Byron stopped the wagon in the shade of the barn, and soon Billy handed around glasses of Kool-Aid.

"Thanks," Aaron breathed.

"Eight hundred sixty-one bales so far."

"Is that good?"

Billy passed Big Danny his Kool-Aid. "It's not a bad day," he allowed.

They sat there, sipping the icy drink.

After getting back his breath, Aaron looked forward to the baler. "How does the knotter work?"

"Guides and needles and ratchets," Billy answered. "It's kinda hard to explain."

Aaron squinted at the complex gears and eyes through which the yellow twine wound itself. "I ask because the knot on the right side of each bale is looser than the knot on the left side. I'd guess there's an adjustment?"

Billy reached for the nearest bale and tested

its twines. Sure enough, the right-side knot was dangerously loose. He went to the baler and with a small wrench began the adjustment. Aaron followed him. "You sure you weren't raised on a farm?" Billy asked him as he worked.

"Maybe in a past life," Aaron said.

Billy glanced sideways at him.

"Sometimes I think that, in a previous existence, I might have been a peasant in central Europe or Russia."

"Probably you just had a good shop teacher in school," Billy said, turning back to his work.

"Shop?" Aaron asked.

"Welding, mechanics, auto body, that kind of stuff."

"We don't have that at Highland Academy," Aaron said. "It's more of a college prep school."

"I thought you said it was a high school."

"It is. A private high school. Most of the kids—ninety-four percent, to be specific—go on to college."

"Well ain't that swell," Billy muttered. He finished the adjustment on the knotter and returned to his Kool-Aid.

"What about you?" Aaron said. "What college are you thinking of?"

Billy laughed once, a brief, harsh sound. He stared off across the farm. "I ain't thinking of any college."

Aaron was quiet. "It doesn't hurt to speculate. . . ."

"College ain't for me," Billy said. "You maybe, but not me."

"I wouldn't necessarily say that—" Aaron began.

Billy interrupted him by draining his glass and standing up to check the sky. "Let's get moving," he said. "Sitting around 'speculating' doesn't put hay in the barn."

At day's end, Aaron's parents arrived. They made him take off most of his clothes and shake out the alfalfa leaves and dust before they'd allow him in the car. Standing there shirtless and with his pants down, Aaron Goldberg looked thinner still, like a skinned rabbit. His arms were scratched in a red corduroy pattern, and as his parents drove him away, Billy doubted that he'd be back. Billy had given him enough farm "experience" to last him a lifetime.

The next morning, wearing his work gloves, there, again, was Aaron Goldberg.

"We could go fishing, even water-skiing," Mrs. Goldberg implored her son as he stiffly exited their station wagon. "Your father would pay someone to take you water-skiing."

"I dislike fishing, and water-skiing strikes me as dangerous," Aaron said in his even, mathematical voice.

"Dangerous? Farming is dangerous. Terrible accidents happen on farms. There are sharp objects, tires to run over you, poisonous insects—" Jacob Goldberg interjected.

"I'm careful, Father," Aaron replied. "Besides,"

he added as he looked about the Baggses' farm, "I like it here."

"My son—the farmer!" Rita Goldberg said, throwing up her hands. "Come on, Jacob, let's go play shuffleboard."

"Good-bye," Aaron said absently to his parents, and headed across the yard to the baler.

By the time Billy had crossed the yard, Aaron was bent over the baler.

"Remarkable technology, really," he said to Billy as he inspected the shiny auger, the pickup reel. "The design is straightforward but not overengineered."

"I guess," Billy allowed.

He watched Aaron touch the baler parts one by one.

"You want something to do?" Billy said. He fished from the twine box the baler's parts-and-service manual. It was a dusty, oil-spotted magazine, and he turned to the lubrication pages, which detailed the locations of each of the thirty-some grease fittings. "Here. Take a look at this." Aaron leaned in quickly to study the diagram.

Billy fetched the grease gun and handed it to Aaron, who hefted the shiny metal tube; he examined its lever handle, its flexible hose, its purple grease.

"Give each fitting two long squirts, or until grease comes out the sides," Billy instructed.

"Understood," Aaron said. He surveyed the book, then the baler.

"Logically, I'll start with what appear to be the most difficult grease-fitting locations."

"Suit yourself," Billy said.

As the kid went quickly to work, Billy scratched his head. Greasing the equipment was one of the dustiest, dirtiest, knuckle-bangingest jobs on the farm. Today as Aaron worked, a tuneless, happy whistling rose from underneath the baler.

"Weird," Billy said to Skinner as they headed back to the barn, "he's a very weird kid."

Later, when Billy returned, Aaron was just finishing up; he worked the grease-gun arm like a pro.

Billy scrutinized his work. He looked for missed fittings but found none. "Looks decent," he said finally.

"Thank you," Aaron said proudly. He turned to Billy. "You know what? At this moment I might well be the happiest I have been in some time."

Billy stared at him.

"Perhaps in years," Aaron added.

"You're strange, you know that, Goldberg? Strange."

"Yes," Aaron said without a pause. "I've been aware that I was different from most boys since I was quite small."

"But as long as you keep workin', I don't mind havin' you around," Billy said, and spit to the side.

Aaron smiled. It was the biggest smile Billy had seen from this kid.

"Come on," Billy said. "I'll show you how to splice one bale of twine to another. We're gonna need plenty of twine. You thought yesterday was tough? Yesterday we was only warming up to bale hay."

By late Wednesday there were 1300 bales of fresh, dry hay in the Baggses' loft and none left in the field. It was time to think of other things. But not baseball.

Not yet.

It was Stretchy Billy had to worry about.

She had stopped milking two weeks ago. She had stopped eating a couple of days ago. Now she hung about listlessly; she did not follow the other cows out to the pasture.

The veterinarian came for a look. Wallace Stevenson was a slow-moving, deliberate man with ruddy cheeks who wore a rubber apron with many round, black patches on it. Aaron Goldberg watched, unblinking, as the Doc donned an arm-length latex glove, then squirted corn oil on it and smeared the lubricant around. Afterward he hoisted Stretchy's tail and slowly inserted his arm deep into her rectum. Staring off over her spine, the Doc silently probed inside the old cow.

Stretchy mooed and showed her yellow teeth to Billy.

"Not good," the doc said as he removed his arm. He peeled off the glove with a snapping sound. After that he knelt and, with one ear pressed to her white, dusty belly, tapped his knuckles all around the distended swell of Stretchy's belly.

Afterward he stood up and began to put away his gear. "Twisted stomach," he said. "At her age there's not much to be done."

Billy was silent. Then he said, "I appreciate your coming by. How much do I owe you?"

The old doc smiled slightly. "I never mind coming to the Baggs farm," he said, closing the rear doors of his truck, "because I know I'll get paid."

Billy handed him one of Abner's twenty-dollar bills and waited for the receipt.

"What are you gonna do with her?" the vet said at length. Billy knew that Doc Stevenson knew Abner was in jail, that Billy was in charge. Everybody knew.

"South Saint Paul, I guess," Billy said, setting his jaw.

"I would," the vet said softly. "I would."

His pen scraped in the silence, and then he tore out the receipt. "You want me to call the trucker? I think he's headed down this afternoon with a load."

Billy looked at Stretchy. He swallowed. There was a long silence in the dusty corral.

"Call him," Billy said abruptly.

In the cab of his truck the veterinarian got on his two-way radio, and in a couple of minutes the arrangements were made. "He'll be here within the hour," the vet said. "You're his last stop."

There was little else to say.

The old vet looked from Billy to Aaron. "Who's your buddy?"

"Goldberg. Aaron Goldberg," Aaron said, stepping forward to shake hands.

Bemused, the old veterinarian shook Aaron's hand. Then he nodded and drove off, already looking down at his clipboard, already thinking about his next stop.

The two boys and Skinner waited for the trucker.

"South Saint Paul?" Aaron said.

"The stockyards," Billy said. "The slaughter-house."

Aaron stared at Stretchy.

"They'll grind her up for hamburger," Billy added, watching Aaron. "Use her bones for meal, her hooves for glue." Maybe that would shut him up for once.

"A productive cow until the end," Goldberg observed.

Billy grabbed Goldberg by the shirt and hoisted him into the air. "What the hell do you know about cows or anything!" He was shouting, near to punching Goldberg.

Aaron Goldberg did not blink. His feet dangled in the air. He just kept looking at Billy in that infuriating, mathematical way. "I didn't mean to upset you."

Billy tossed him aside, where Aaron tumbled

to the ground and sprawled in the dust. Slowly he got up and brushed himself off. Billy went over to the corral fence. He leaned on the rail and stared at Stretchy. Aaron followed.

"She was a good cow," Billy muttered. "A damn good cow." Then he didn't say any more because he didn't trust his voice.

They were silent awhile, both of them leaning on the fence.

Then Aaron said, "I'll bet it's like being a baseball manager. Say you have a veteran player, a former top producer, and a nice person besides. Then you have to release him."

"Something like that," Billy said.

"Maybe getting to be friends is the mistake."

Billy glared at Aaron. "Yeah, maybe it damn well is."

After that the two of them waited there, by the corral, in silence for a long time. Finally, up the road came the dust and rattle and faint mooing from the cattle truck.

After the truck and Stretchy were gone, Billy headed to the Baggses' pickup. "Get in," he said.

Aaron did. "Ah . . . where are we going?"

"To town."

"Do you have a driver's license?"

"Does the pope have a wife?"

Aaron shrugged. Then he looked around the cab.

"What? What the hell you looking for?"

"Is there a seat belt?"

Billy laughed derisively, then accelerated sharply down the driveway. Aaron hung on to the door handle.

"Would this be considered a 'joy ride'?" Aaron asked.

Billy careened onto the highway. "Yeah," Billy said, speeding up still more. "That's what it is. A joy ride."

They rattled along at full tilt. The wind and noise gradually blew away some of Billy's anger, and slowly he reduced their speed.

"Actually, there is one task we should do in town," Aaron ventured.

"Like what?"

"Scouting. We need to scout the Town Team."

Billy spit out the window and drove on. "I know the Town Team. I played on it last year."

"But I've never seen them," Aaron countered.

Billy swore briefly and spit again out the window. Goldberg: the kid who was always right.

At the edge of the picnic area, and just across from the Feedmill, Billy stopped the truck. Aaron got out. He had a small, pocket-sized notepad and a pen.

"You carry that everywhere?"

Aaron nodded.

"Strange," Billy said.

"But practical," Aaron answered, with a trace of a smile. He squinted across to the ball field, where boys shouted and the coach's bat went *crack!* "I was thinking—since they know you, I had best go alone."

"Fine by me," Billy said. "You scout. I've got to go visit my old man."

Aaron was silent.

"He lives in town," Billy said.

Aaron blinked. "I had noticed the absence of your father," he said, "but I thought it best not to ask."

"Go ahead. Ask me."

"I presume there was a divorce?"

"Wrong," Billy said with some pleasure. "He's in jail."

Aaron's eyes widened slightly.

"He killed a man."

"He did?"

"Yup. With an axe."

Aaron swallowed, and quickly set off to scout the Town Team. Billy laughed as he watched Goldberg hurry away. Twice he looked back over his shoulder at Billy, who made a chopping motion with his arm. Goldberg's eyes widened.

Billy laughed again as Goldberg continued toward the field. There a few people sat in the stands, the mothers reading paperbacks and their children climbing on the wooden bleachers; at ground level were the usual town-type fathers, standing along the fence calling directions to their sons. Aaron eased up alongside the dugout completely unnoticed. In some ways he was the most unnoticeable kid Billy had ever met, and in other ways the most bothersome. But hell, Billy thought, no kid was perfect. And if Goldberg wasn't Robert, he was some company at least.

Billy lit a cigarette and drove uptown. He no longer coughed when he smoked, and he didn't mind the taste either. Turning north, he cruised slowly through the tidy suburb of Green Lawn. Then onto Venus Lane. It was midafternoon and the Langen house was quiet. No one splashed in the backyard pool. No one moved past the big picture window. The whole neighborhood was quiet.

Back on Main Street Billy drove even slower and shaded his eyes so that he could see into the café and into Schinder's Malt Shop. On this hot summer afternoon there were tourists aplenty, but no tall girl with a platinum ponytail and shiny, golden legs.

Billy turned the pickup toward the riverfront and parked in the far corner of the beach parking lot. Beyond the stone changing house, at the water's edge, he could hear the hoot and splash of kids. Rows of bicycles filled the iron racks.

Acting casual, Billy eased up to the side of the old fieldstone building and leaned there, smoking a fresh one. The grass in front was staked out by mothers on blankets with their toddlers. Closer to the water was yellow sand and teen-agers, who raced and threw Frisbees. At water's edge was the old concrete platform; kids raced off it, bicycling their legs madly before splashing down, while others waited, shivering, in line at the diving board for their turn to jackknife high, then slice straight into the silty blue water. He watched the divers. Billy was a lousy swimmer. Most farm kids swam like stones.

Squinting against the brilliant light, he scanned the beach for sight of Suzy Langen. He looked among the divers, among the Frisbee throwers, among the tanners. No Suzy.

About to leave, he noticed, off to the far side, several wheelchairs parked by the shore. A nurse in white pants and top stood there among the nodding, drooling occupants of the chairs. Re-tarded folks, the most disabled ones, from the Flint Group Home. Their chairs were lined up in a row, and the one nearest the water was empty. In the water, flailing about, moaning with pleasure, was a very fat man with a very small head. Helping him, guiding him, making sure he didn't drown, was Suzy Langen.

Billy swallowed; the cool stone building felt suddenly heavy against his shoulder.

There was Suzy in the water in her white bathing suit working with the retards.

Watching her, he felt a heavy, rank sweat start to come on his body. He felt his knees go weak, his ears ring, his heart begin to flop like an out-of-balance tire, his tongue go dry; the cigarette began to shake in his hands—he ditched the damn smoke before he burned himself, then stood there watching her.

He watched her lift the fat man back to his chair, then buckle him. He watched her smile at the man, pat his shoulder. As she stood fully erect, Billy had the craziest of all sensations, one that hit him like a lightning strike: someday he and Suzy Langen—

"Hey, Billy!" a voice shrilled.

It was Tiny Tim Loren skidding up on his bicycle.

Billy saw Suzy Langen look up—look his way.

"What are you doing here, Billy?" Tim said excitedly.

"Public beach," Billy muttered. "And what are you doing here? You're supposed to be at base-ball practice."

"I'm skipping."

"Well, you better not," Billy warned. "In case you haven't heard, you've got a serious ball game this Friday night." He kept glancing back toward the beach. Suzy kept looking his way.

"I heard," Tim said. "That's why I'm skipping. If I don't make the practices, the coach won't play me, and then I won't have to bat against you, Billy." Tiny Tim grinned.

"Sure," Billy said sarcastically. Then he figured out that Tim was telling the truth. He focused his attention on him. "Get your ass back to practice, because I need to know what's going on with the Town Team."

"You want me to spy?" Tim said.

"I didn't say 'spy.'"

Tim grinned. "But that's what you meant."

Billy shrugged. "King and everybody, are they all going to be there Friday night?"

"What's in it for me if I tell you?" Tim teased, staying just out of Billy's reach.

Billy thought a moment. "Friday night I'll give you one fat pitch."

"Cross your heart? Poke a stick in your dick?"

Billy nodded.

"All right, I'm your spy," Tim said. "Yes—everybody's gonna be there, and Kenwood's having a party at his house afterward—a victory party, he calls it."

"Is that so?" Billy said sarcastically. Suddenly, behind him, Suzy Langen approached. She was drying herself with a towel and milking water from her ponytail.

"Hello, Billy," she said, securing the towel around her waist. Water shone in those little hollows above her collarbones.

"Suzy," he managed to reply. His voice went half squeaky; he didn't know quite where to look at her, so he chose a spot in the air beside her right ear.

"I suppose you two are talking about the big game?" she said teasingly.

"Big game?"

"At your farm. Friday night. Everybody in town knows about it."

"Really?" Billy said dumbly.

"Really," she said with a smile.

"It's true," Tiny Tim said. "The County Fair is over. What else is there to do in a dipshit town like Flint?"

"I'm hoping to come," Suzy said to Billy.

"You are?" Billy looked straight at her for the first time. He felt his stomach do a combination jackknife and belly flop. "To the farm?"

She nodded. "If that's all right."

"Ah . . . no, no, of course not—I mean I don't mind."

"Good," she said easily.

"So who are you gonna cheer for?" Tiny Tim quizzed Suzy. "Town Team or Farm Team?"

"I haven't decided yet," she said.

Billy's knees turned to rubber; the whole beach seemed to tilt. Luckily Suzy glanced back to the nurse, who was lining up the caravan of wheelchairs. "Well, I've got to get back to work."

"That's your summer job?" Billy said stupidly.

"Yes, why?"

"I dunno," Billy said. "I thought you probably didn't have to work." Then his face reddened; the words had just slipped out.

"Maybe I don't," Suzy said sharply, "but since I hate asking my parents for money, I do."

"Why work with those retards?" Tiny Tim said. "Uggh!"

Suzy shrugged. "I get to be outside a lot. And they're nice, gentle people."

Tim shuddered. "You'd never catch me working with feebs."

"What if you were mentally handicapped?" Suzy said, hands on her hips.

"I know one thing."

"What's that?" Suzy said.

"I'd definitely want you to give me my baths," Tim replied.

"And I'd definitely use very cold water," Suzy shot back as she headed off.

Billy watched her long legs and her bare feet move her across the concrete. She still dripped river water; she left a trail.

"See you Friday night, Billy," she called back over her shoulder.

Billy held up one hand in a weak farewell wave. The sun suddenly felt intensely hot. Sweat ran down his spine. "Jesus! What am I going to do?" he murmured.

"Make out with her in the hayloft after the game?" Tim ventured.

Billy turned and balled a fist, but Tiny Tim was already leaping onto his bike. "Remember," he called back as he headed to baseball practice, "one fat pitch—you promised."

Billy drove straightaway to Doctors' Clinic.

"Billy!" said Mavis with surprise. She wore her

good blue dress and sat straight-backed at her desk typing; he was always astounded at how different she looked away from the farm. It made him tongue-tied.

"Everything all right?"

He nodded.

"Good," she said with relief. "Come on back. There might be a sweet roll left over."

Billy followed his mother through the waiting room, which was filled with mothers and their squalling babies, and people with various coughs and bandages. Ahead in the hallway a nurse, wide in her white uniform, came out of the small lunchroom licking her fingers.

"Then again, maybe the sweet rolls are all gone," Mavis said loudly to Billy.

The nurse glared at Mavis.

Once they were inside, alone, Billy spoke to his mother. "Ma, we got to talk."

"About what, Billy?"

"The game. Friday night."

"What about it?"

"Everybody's talking about it."

"So?"

"So all sorts of people might be coming."

"That's good."

"I mean, lots of people," Billy said. "From town."

"Come one, come all," Mavis said. Then she smiled. "I'm sure it will be mainly the Town Team and a few parents. People aren't going to drive

twenty miles to see a baseball game in somebody's pasture, Billy."

"Maybe you're right," Billy said. He calmed
down somewhat, and began to munch on a dry
cookie.

Just then Doctor Lloyd, the silvery-haired
physician, swept into the room for a cup of coffee
on the run. "Master Baggs," he said with a smile,
and shook hands.

"Hullo!" Billy said. The doctor, with his
fine-boned fingers and straight teeth and gray-
blue eyes, always made Billy feel backward and
clumsy and misdressed.

"By the way, good luck Friday night," he said
to Billy.

Billy glanced quickly to Mavis.

"If I'm not on call at the hospital, I'll try to be
there," the doctor said.

Mavis's mouth slacked half open.

"Good doctors keep their ears open," Doctor
Lloyd said to Mavis with a teasing smile. "That's
what my patients are talking about this week—
the big game Friday night at the Baggs farm."

"Goodness!" Mavis murmured.

But Doctor Lloyd was gone by then, and she
and Billy were left to stare at each other.

Billy stopped briefly at the jail to see Abner.

"So what's new on the home place?" Abner
asked, watching Billy carefully.

"Stretchy," Billy said, and told his father the
details. Afterward he waited for Abner's reaction,

for his complaint about the vet's bill.

"Sounds like the right move," Abner said, and Billy let out a breath. "Anything else?"

Billy faked a yawn. "Nothing at all. Just cows in the morning and cows at night—how about you, Pa?"

"How about me what?" Abner said suspiciously.

"Anything new goin' on?"

"Does it look like it?" Abner said, gesturing to his cell door. "The sheriff tried to talk to Langen, told him I paid Meyers, but it was like pissing into the wind."

Happily exiting the jail—at least Abner had not heard about the big game—Billy headed back to the Feedmill and ball field. Aaron Goldberg spotted him and came back to the truck. Before Aaron had swung himself fully into the pickup, Billy accelerated down the street.

"What's the hurry?" Aaron called as he hung on for his life.

"It's Wednesday afternoon. We've got two and a half days to get ready for the big game."

"Don't you want to hear my scouting report?"

"Later," Billy said, but Aaron gave it to him anyway.

Arriving back at the farm in record time, Billy stopped the truck midway up the driveway. He stared over the farm, at the cluttered yard.

"Spectator parking, yes," Aaron said, "I've already thought of that."

"Huh?" Billy shot a look sideways to Goldberg.

"Will this work?" Aaron withdrew from his clipboard a map showing cars parked in even rows along the garden and the driveway. It was drawn to scale: fifty to one. "We'll need someone to direct traffic. From talk at the ball field I'm guessing there will be up to one hundred cars."

"A hundred cars?" Billy murmured.

"It's best to be prepared," Aaron said. "There's also the problem of spectator seating. I figure that the hayracks would be perfect. Three hayracks plus bales stacked in ascending rows, with a capacity of fifty people per wagon. They'll be just like bleachers," Aaron said, presenting Billy with another drawing, "plus they're portable. We can move them anywhere we like."

Billy scanned the drawing.

"And one other matter is public sanitation," Aaron said. "Did you notice that it's starting to smell a bit rank behind the corncrib?"

"Pissy," Billy murmured. "Yeah, I noticed that. Someone even took a dump back there."

"Could we move the outdoor toilet closer to the ball field?"

"I suppose so, sure. We can use the tractor and loader."

"Good." Aaron checked that off his list. "Also, Gina Erickson actually had an idea," Aaron continued. A faint smile passed through his squinty eyes. "With some slight remodeling we could put all the food concessions under one roof—in the corncrib."

Billy listened.

"Plus we should formalize the food end of things a bit," Aaron added. "Are there any catering clubs, any groups around here that do that sort of thing?"

"What's catering?"

"It's a food business, food delivered."

Billy scratched his head. "There's the 4-H Club, that or the Lutheran Ladies' Aid; they do a lotta funerals."

"The Lutheran Ladies sound perfect," Aaron said.

Billy gave him a couple of names.

"I'll make the call," Aaron said, and checked CONCESSIONS off his list, "which leaves mainly the backstop screen and some light grounds work."

"Sure," Billy said abstractedly. He had turned back to stare over the farm. He had been seeing the Baggs farm as Suzy Langen might see it: a narrow white house in need of paint. Mavis's dead Chevy. A barn that used to be red but now was mainly weathered boards. The old outbuildings made of slab wood and tar paper. The various ancient farm implements that Abner had cannibalized for parts—all of it had to be painted or cleaned up!

But in the next instant Billy knew that was not possible. Not the lifetime of a farm in two and a half days. Suzy Langen and the other people from town would just have to like it or lump it. He felt some of the old anger, the old stubbornness, the old pride begin to well up inside him like stomach acid, like bile.

Aaron, however, in his even, mathematical voice, got Billy back on track. "So," he said, "what do you want to work on first?"

B y Friday noon, two plank benches were in place alongside the first and third baselines. One was marked VISITORS and the other FARM TEAM.

The hayracks with bale bleachers were towed into position just behind the players' benches.

Spectator parking was laid out, with the garden and lawn cordoned off with twine and ribbons, with parking signs pointing their arrows along the lane. There was plenty of overflow parking available in the hayfield beside the ball diamond.

The outhouse was set over a freshly dug hole near the field, and NO PISSING (OR ANYTHING ELSE) signs were tacked onto the back of the corncrib and behind the other outbuildings.

With Billy working the chain saw and Aaron pounding nails, the corncrib had been quickly remodeled to offer an open window and long plank counter. Electricity, not just a cord but an actual overhead line, ran from the barn and down into the crib, where Billy at the moment was securing the last of the outlets.

"Where did you learn how to do that?" Aaron asked; he looked over Billy's shoulder at the wiring.

"From my old man," Billy said. He tightened the final wire nut.

"He must know how to do nearly everything."

"Yup," Billy said.

"Too bad he can't be here for the game," Aaron said.

Billy turned to Aaron. "Are you kidding?"

Aaron blinked. "Doesn't he like baseball?"

Billy shrugged and returned to his work. "He likes baseball okay, but he sure as hell wouldn't like it here. He don't like commotion, or strangers around."

Aaron was silent a moment. "What if he finds out?"

"He'd whup my ass."

Aaron thought about that. "It seems likely that he'll hear about the game at some point. Flint is not that big a town."

"He might hear about it, but not from me. Anyway, what can he do right now?"

"True . . ." Aaron admitted.

Billy was pleased to have the upper hand of logic for once. "Plus, by the time he gets out of jail, I'll have everything changed back the way it was," Billy added.

Aaron stared. "Even the field?"

Billy stared again at the diamond. He had no answer to that question. Maybe he would take a chance and keep the field; on the other hand, that might get him a double whupping when Abner came home.

"Come on," Billy said, "we've got to finish the backstop."

As Billy worked high on the upraised tractor's scoop, nailing chicken wire to the post, a glint of light from the road caught his eye. He squinted. The flash was sunlight off the windshield of a long white car. The car stopped and remained parked by the mailbox. A woman drove; there were two kids in back.

"Aaron, go onto the porch and get the binoculars," he said. He kept pounding staples.

In a minute Aaron returned.

"Step off to the side and check out the road. There's a white car."

Aaron climbed into the hay shed and steadied the glasses. "It's a Cadillac. Convertible. There's a woman with short hair driving and two boys in back."

"Is there a dark-haired kid looking this way?"

"Yes."

"Is there a waterski in the backseat?"

"Yes," Aaron said with surprise. "It looks like they've been to the beach."

Billy nodded and rose to stare at the car. "Any half-assed baseball scout should recognize the dark-haired kid."

Aaron was silent; he adjusted the focus. "It's King Kenwood!" he said suddenly.

Billy dropped his hammer and turned his back to the road. "Tell me if this gets any reaction." In one motion he lowered his pants and his undershorts and bent over low.

Aaron, squinting through the binoculars, began to wheeze with laughter.

Billy grinned evilly and held his pose.

"I should mention," Aaron said, "that King's mother has binoculars, too."

"What!" Billy's mouth came open. He yanked up his pants as the Cadillac lurched forward and sped off in a cloud of dust. "No way!"

"It's true," Aaron hooted, and began to laugh like crazy. He collapsed onto the hay bales in an actual, real-life, totally normal teenage laughing fit.

For not telling him about Mrs. Kenwood's binoculars, Billy made Aaron clean the gutter and scrape the barn alley while he himself fed silage and got the milking machine ready. Aaron wrinkled his nose at the odors, but kept shoveling and scraping. And at four o'clock Billy turned on the compressor. "Sorry, girls," he called to the two rows of Holsteins as they mooed and fidgeted in their stanchions. "I know it's early, but I want all of you long gone to pasture by five o'clock."

And, an hour later, Billy was just opening the back barn door to let out the cows when the first vehicle arrived.

"It's Ole Svendson," Aaron said.

"Put him to work," Billy said.

Aaron was happy to take charge, as was Ole. The bachelor farmer straightened his shoulders, his spine and his cap at his new job: chief parking attendant. "There's one already," he said, pointing down the road. But it was just Mrs. Pederson letting off Mavis.

She walked briskly up the lane.

"Hi, everybody," she called. "My—doesn't it look tidy around here!"

Billy shrugged but had to smile. Aaron had mowed the grass around the buildings, plus carted away stray lumber, barrels and pails. Billy had towed two old tractors and a gutted combine back behind the sawmill. And Mavis's Chevy as well.

She looked at the spot where the Chevy had been. Only an oil stain remained on the paler grass.

"We should have done that sooner," she murmured. Then she reclaimed her smile and checked her watch. "We'd better hurry and eat," she said. "Ole, have you had supper?"

"No time for that," Ole said, staring down the road.

After supper, Mavis sent Aaron with a plate of food for Ole, who had lined up several of the earliest-arriving cars, mainly members of the Farm Team and the Lutheran Ladies' Auxiliary Club. Inside the corncrib a tinny-sounding radio played country music, and behind the slats several small, blue-haired ladies moved back and forth. They chatted and set out trays of brownies and sliced buns, while others began to heat up the hot-dog rotisserie and affix wieners to the wires; still others worked at loading the big popcorn popper with corn, oil and butter, while the smallest of the Lutheran Ladies inked in prices of all the food items on a signboard in shaky but clear cursive.

Aaron and Billy ran the last of the white lines on the ball field and raked the mound into a perfect, low dome.

"Now what?" Billy said. His stomach was jumping inside. He shouldn't have eaten supper so fast. And he kept wondering when—or if—Suzy Langen would arrive.

Aaron checked his clipboard. "Nothing," he said. "It's time now we concentrated on winning this ball game."

Billy looked at Aaron, then once more about the farm: They would not be at all ready for this game were it not for Aaron Goldberg.

"One last thing," Aaron began, almost apologetically.

"What's that?"

"The Farm Team needs a coach."

"Yes, I guess it does . . ." Billy said. He kept his face poker straight.

Aaron leaned forward slightly. "It's the one thing we haven't done," Aaron said, "choose a coach."

"True," Billy said, scratching his head, pretending that he could think of no one quite right for the job. "We sure do need a coach."

Aaron fidgeted.

"Unless . . ." Billy looked up.

Aaron smiled eagerly.

"No, my mother wouldn't work," Billy said.

"True," Aaron said, with a slight note of relief in his voice.

"Hey—" Billy said, "why not you?"

"Me?"

"Yeah, you, Goldberg."

"Me as actual head coach?"

Billy nodded.

"Me?" Goldberg repeated.

"I mean, if you don't want to—"

"No, no—I didn't mean to imply that," Aaron said quickly.

"So what do you say?"

Goldberg's nose began to twitch, his Adam's apple to bob up and down, his eyes to water.

"Now what's the matter with you?" Billy exclaimed. "You ain't gonna cry!"

"I could. It's possible," Goldberg said, attempting to maintain his even, mathematical voice.

"Why in the hell for?!"

"Because this clearly is the happiest moment of my life."

"Oh no—not that again," Billy groaned.

Aaron recovered himself by reaching for his clipboard and flipping through its pages. In a few moments he had composed himself. "Actually, I did take the liberty of making up the Farm Team batting order," he said.

By six o'clock all the Farm Team players, including the González brothers, had arrived; Billy let out a sigh of relief as their loaded-down station wagon came up the dusty driveway. Aaron Goldberg blew his whistle (which he had had all the while in his pocket), and the Farm Team gathered around.

"What! Is *he* going to be coach?" Gina Erickson asked, and wrinkled her nose at Aaron (who did smell barny).

"Shut up and listen," Billy growled.

"The batting order looks like this," Aaron said. He read off the names and positions.

> Raúl González — second base
> Jesús González — shortstop
> Shawn Howenstein — third base
> Billy Baggs — pitcher
> Danny Boyer — left field
> Owen McGinty — first base
> Bob McGinty — center field
> Gina Erickson — right field
> Heather Erickson — catcher

"Raúl bats first because he's got a nice small strike zone but a sweet swing," Aaron explained. "Jesús is a contact hitter and obviously works well next to his brother. Shawn and Billy have good power to bring home some RBIs. I'm putting Danny fifth because, with any luck, King Kenwood will have just given up a hit or two, and be vulnerable in the area of control; and Danny, of course, will be taking all the way."

The Farm Team players looked at each other—then nodded and murmured their agreement. Even Gina Erickson shrugged.

"Owen and Bob are free swingers," Aaron said. "They'll try to get on base any way they can.

"Gina and Heather, just get your bat out there in plenty of time and try to make contact. We've worked on bunting. Don't be afraid to lay one down."

Heather, rocking her baby, nodded confidently.

"And then we're back to the top of the order," Aaron said, but his voice changed to one of concern. "You'll note that we have no substitute players, so don't get injured."

"Why not put Skinner on the roster?" Gina Erickson joked. "He can catch the ball good as anyone."

The Farm Team had a good laugh as they headed out to take the infield; Aaron Goldberg, however, stared at the dog. "What the heck," he muttered, and penciled in Skinner's name at the bottom.

With the Farm Team on the field, and Coach Goldberg watching as Billy hit fungoes, a shiny new motor home came creaking up the driveway. It was a long, square-faced Winnebago that was directed by Ole Svendson into the hayfield toward the VISITORS side.

"Stay focused," Goldberg called to his players, but Billy's eyes kept turning to the motor home. Inside there was laughing and shouting—then down its steel steps, one by one, came the Town Team.

Which separated itself into two groups. One included Billy's friends Dusty Streeter, Butch Redbird, Jake the Fake Robertson and Tiny Tim, who all came over to the fence to admire the field. The other town group consisted of Kenwood's friends; they stood pointing and snickering at the chicken-wire backstop, at the hayrack bleachers, at the outhouse.

The driver, Mark Kenwood, strode briskly onto the field. "Who's in charge here?" he called out, looking around for an adult.

"Me," Aaron Goldberg said. "Second base," he ordered Billy, and Billy cracked a grounder to Raúl.

Mark Kenwood stared. "You? You're the coach?" King stood to the side, watching.

"That's right. Aaron Goldberg's the name."

Mark Kenwood shrugged. "I brought my motor home. I didn't know what . . . facilities you had out here. You know, bathrooms, that sort of thing."

"Fine," Aaron said. "There's plenty of parking room."

"Facilities?" Billy remarked from the side of

his mouth. "Usually 'out here' we just shit in the woods."

Butch Redbird and Dusty Streeter snickered. King came up to the fence to watch the Farm Team players; he watched them carefully. In the midst of this a small roar and rattle came up the driveway, and Coach Anderson braked his Toyota to a halt behind the motor home. "What are you guys standing around for?" he called out his window to the Town Team. "Start warming up."

Reluctantly, Butch Redbird and the rest of Billy's friends rejoined the Town Team.

"Warm up?" said one of King's friends. "We aren't gonna break a sweat tonight." There was general laughter.

"Infield, take two," Aaron Goldberg called, and rapped one to the left side. Shawn scooped the hard grounder and threw to second, where Raúl bounded high in the air, like a fawn soaring over a tree stump, for the relay to first.

The smile on Mark Kenwood's face slipped a notch.

"Take two, Jesús," Aaron called. Jesús fielded a tidy backhand, went all glove for the relay to Raúl, who smoked it, sidearmed, to first.

Mark Kenwood's smile disappeared altogether. He looked to King, whispered something; King's eyes had already narrowed.

"Was that you scouting today in the white Caddy?" Billy called over to King.

"Maybe," King said.

"See anything interesting?"

King turned on his heel and trotted back to the Town Team. "Let's go!" he called. "Get loose! Move the ball!"

"Sure, King," someone called lazily.

"Shut up. I'm telling you—get focused," King shouted. There was anger and a note of urgency in his voice.

Coach Anderson only smiled.

Gradually the Town Team's laughter and jiving quieted as its members began to look more closely at the Farm Team.

"Who are those cats at second and short?" someone murmured.

"The González brothers. From Mexico."

"Mexico!"

"Where, as you can no doubt see, they play baseball all year round," Coach Anderson added.

The Town Team was silent.

"Well, they might have an infield, but dig the outfield," someone offered. The town boys watched as a fly ball lit within arm's reach of motionless Big Danny. Their laughter returned. "A retard, a sheep farmer and a girl."

"Stay focused," King said.

"Sure, King, sure . . ."

"Pretend we're playing Buckman," King said.

"Buckwheat?"

"Bucktooth?"

"Butthole?"

There was laughter as the Town Team fell

back to its lackadaisical, goof-off ways—all, surprisingly, except Tiny Tim Loren, who threw energetically and kept his mouth shut.

Even Billy noticed Tim, who grinned and held up one finger to Billy. "Remember . . ." he mouthed.

"Maybe," Billy called back.

"You promised," Tim said.

Cars continued to come up the driveway and send up pale, fine flowers of dust that gathered and blossomed in the evening sunlight. A tawny glow began to fall over the field and the swelling crowd. Ole Svendson, with a cattle cane as a pointer, directed traffic like a New York City policeman. "Left! Right! Pull straight ahead!" One by the one the vehicles kept coming. Farm pickups, town cars, even a few tourist cars with out-of-state license plates turned in and parked in orderly rows.

"Pull ahead! Keep moving. You can't stop there!" Ole called, waving his imposing cane.

Among the vehicles was Dale Schwartz's El Camino. "He's here!" Gina said.

Heather narrowed her eyes.

Billy watched Schwartz park at the far end of the row, then join the spectators along the fence. Schwartz winked at Heather, who turned quickly away.

"You okay?" Billy asked Heather.

"I'm fine," she answered, and pegged the ball on a hard line to Billy.

"You want me to, I'll take a ball bat after him."

"No," Heather said sharply. "I got my own game plan."

Billy shrugged and left her alone.

As Billy sat to watch the Town Team take the infield, Shawn Howenstein poked his ribs and jerked his head toward the stands.

Billy turned and went numb. Standing in the dust and sunlight, wearing white shorts and a white sleeveless blouse, standing a head taller than the other girls with her, was Suzy Langen. She stood exactly behind the home-plate screen.

Not only Suzy, but behind her, wearing a sun visor, was none other than Mrs. Langen. She was staring over her shoulder at the Baggses' farm pickup.

"Shit—" Billy murmured.

"Not here," Shawn said, leaning away.

"Shut up," Billy muttered, keeping his eye on Suzy without being obvious. Billy saw her watching the Town Team, saw her wave to King Kenwood and a couple other town kids. Then she spotted Billy on the Farm Team bench. Through her eyes Billy saw the Farm Team. They were a ragged bunch of kids, some without baseball caps, some with homemade leather gloves, kids ranging in size from the deer-thin González brothers to the stubby Erickson girls to the gigantic Danny Boyer—and not to forget Skinner, tied to the far end of the bench, who wagged his tail and barked each time the ball was batted.

Suzy waved once to Billy.

Billy nodded briefly. His stomach did a full back flip. He felt sweat come onto his forehead.

"Who is that girl?" Aaron said, casting a long look Billy's way.

"Nobody," Billy said immediately.

Aaron raised one eyebrow. "If she's nobody, try not to think about her until after the game," he said in his coach's voice.

Billy spit between his shoes. "Why in hell did I make him head coach?" he muttered to no one in particular.

But Aaron didn't hear Billy. He was looking behind Suzy Langen to some other arrivals. "And if I'm not mistaken, guess who else is here."

Billy looked—and froze for real this time. Beside the sheriff's car stood Sheriff Harvey Olson, Mavis and a tall, dark man in orange coveralls: Billy's father. Mavis had her arm happily around Abner, who stood with his jaw dropped nearly to his chest as he stared at the field, at the crowd.

Billy whirled to look beyond the outfield fence, to the far timber. In a few minutes he could be deep into the woods and headed west, to North Dakota—hell, clear to California.

"Your father didn't really murder someone," Aaron said.

"How do you know?" Billy muttered, still staring Abner's way.

"Axe murderers don't get let out to attend baseball games."

Billy shrugged.

"And no matter what, you'd best go see him," Aaron said, putting a heavy hand on Billy's shoulder. "Do it now, before the game starts." It was weird what a coach's whistle and clipboard did to some people; it was weirder still how other people obeyed them.

Billy slowly hoisted himself from the bench and trudged through the crowd toward his father.

Abner Baggs, in his bright coveralls, blinked and focused his brown eyes on Billy, who kept coming closer, though at a slower and slower pace.

"Hello, Billy," the sheriff called. "Not much doing at the jail tonight, so your father and I took a little evening ride."

"That was awfully nice of you, Sheriff," Mavis said, hugging Abner again.

Abner was too astounded to even worry about being hugged in public. He kept staring at Billy like he was dreaming.

"Hi, Pa," Billy ventured. He stopped just out of arm's reach.

Abner murmured, "Hello, son. . . ." For some weird reason, he reached out to shake hands.

Billy took the proffered hand. He glanced at his mother, then back to Abner. "Big game tonight, Pa."

Abner stared beyond Billy to the corncrib. "There are people, old ladies, in my corncrib," he murmured.

"That's right," Mavis said.

"Old ladies making popcorn . . ."

"And wieners and coffee," Mavis added. "Are you hungry, Abner?"

"I suppose a little . . ." Abner said in his stunned, faraway voice

"I gotta go, Pa," Billy said.

"Sure, son," Abner murmured as he followed Mavis toward the corncrib.

Back at the field, Aaron Goldberg exchanged rosters with Coach Anderson. "Also we'll need you or the team representative to sign this insurance waiver," Aaron said, holding up his clipboard. "This insulates the Baggs family from any litigation resulting from injury."

Coach Anderson glanced at Billy, then at Mark Kenwood. Kenwood came forward, reviewed the document. "Where'd you get this?"

"My father's an attorney. He carries them everywhere."

Mark Kenwood shrugged. "Looks okay to me."

Coach Anderson signed.

"Also, in the excitement we've forgotten one important item," Aaron said.

"What's that?" Coach Anderson said.

"An umpire."

"I figured I'd do the umpiring," Coach Anderson said.

"That would be a conflict of interest."

Coach laughed. "Son, this is only a scrimmage."

"No, it's a game," Aaron replied. "I distinctly recall that we used the word 'game.'"

The coach scratched his head. Looked around. His eyes fell upon Sheriff Olson.

"Harvey, you used to play ball. We need a plate umpire."

"Me?"

The coach nodded.

"It's been a while," the sheriff said, "but I guess that's kind of what I do in Flint County—umpire."

"Any objections to the sheriff?" the coach said to Goldberg.

"He should do fine. Thank you."

There was scattered clapping from the hayracks as the sheriff unbuckled his gun, stuffed his handcuffs in his back pocket and donned a spare catcher's mask. He reached into his pocket for a coin.

"Call it for home-team advantage," the sheriff said, and spun a dime into the air.

"Heads," Aaron said.

The coin flashed higher and higher, then fell.

The two coaches and the sheriff bent low to look into the dirt.

The sheriff rose. "The Farm Team is home," he called, waving them onto the field. "Let's play ball!"

CHAPTER

26

And the big game? How did it proceed? The answer depends upon your point of view. Consider, for example, the airplane pilot. As the players took the field, high above the Baggs farm was a Beechcraft Queen-Aire, a small cargo plane, heading from Duluth to Grand Forks. On the ground something flashed, bright, like a row of white dominoes falling. The pilot turned his head, then banked his plane for a closer look. A farm. A baseball diamond, the outfield fence lined with tiny black-and-white dairy cows—and rows and rows of parked cars with bright, flashing windshields. The pilot checked his watch, then slipped off several hundred feet of altitude for a closer look. On the diamond the players were in position; they did not look up at the lazily circling plane. The pilot saw the pitcher step sharply toward home plate; saw the batter spin in place. The batter did not run. "Stee-rike," the pilot murmured, and smiled. From two thousand feet he could not of course see the ball, and, at ground level, neither could the batter. The pilot made one more circle, but had a schedule to keep, and reluctantly flew on. . . .

At ground level, the cows leaned on the outfield fence and switched their tails, and quivered the skin on their backs at the blackflies, and chewed their cuds with an unending, sideways grinding motion. Their job was to make milk, which they did well, did twenty-four hours a day, and anything beyond making milk, anything new to look at, was a bonus—especially people who threw balls and cheered. So the cows chewed their cuds and watched without opinions of any kind, and they did not keep score. . . .

The little kids playing hide-and-seek among the rows of parked cars had become bored after the first inning of the big game and turned to their own devices. Something they could play—such as hide-and-seek. Now they crouched, barefooted, on the sharp hay stubble, trembling with hope and fear behind bumpers and beneath transmissions as other bare feet passed slowly along—within inches of their safe spots. For the little kids, the baseball game proceeded in another world, another universe. . . .

In one of the cars were the Haroldson girl and the Keefner boy, both sixteen, locked in a French kiss, making out like crazy in the backseat of somebody's Oldsmobile. All the cars were unlocked, and so they had taken their pick—a large car with a big backseat, that's all they asked. Now they were hoping for a close game, one that held people's attention. Even better would be a game that went extra innings. . . .

The small, old ladies of the Lutheran Auxiliary were too busy to keep score. Besides, they could see the game only vaguely through the dust and glare of the western sunlight. Whenever there was cheering, they peered out between the slats of the corncrib concession stand like tiny barn owls—after which they turned back to their food, not to eat, for none of them consumed much more than a bird these days, but to keep it coming for the customers. As they worked, they talked. They told their stories. Stories about Emma Aylesworth's stroke, about Agnes Gustad at the rest home—how she had struck out walking, and had nearly made it the eight miles back to her home (long vacant now), before someone had spotted her and hauled her back to the old-age home. In the middle of these stories, customers came to the window for refreshments—for popcorn, wieners, pop, brownies, lemonade, coffee—and it was the food and the beverages that brought the old ladies back to the present, to the healthy and to the living. "What inning is it?" the tiny lady at the counter asked each customer.

"Third inning. Farm Team one to nothing."

"The third inning already!" Most of the hot dogs were gone. Now the Lutheran Ladies began to fret about their supply of food. They worried that it would not last until the game was over, that it would not last until the final out. . . .

The very old men who sat on the hayracks or leaned on the fence posts along the ball field looked attentive, but in truth they had come unstuck in time. In the haze and the sunlight and cheers and groans, they squinted and remembered their old days as ballplayers. As soldiers. As lovers. Now that they were old men, time and memories and people played hob in the fields of their minds. It was difficult nowadays to remember who was on first, who had already come home.

A far more attentive fan was Rick Allen, a small, intense man with a baseball cap and a mustache. He was the baseball coach from the nearby town of Buckman, and he had slipped into the farm crowd unnoticed. He made it a point to know what was going on in Flint County, for the towns of Flint and Buckman had long been rivals. Allen was there to scout one player in particular; Billy Baggs. At the end of last summer he had seen this rough farm-boy flamethrower rear back and strike out a side of Buckman Warriors. The Warriors had already won the game, but it did not feel like it after Billy Baggs had humiliated his batters.

"Who *was* that last kid?" Allen had asked Coach Anderson after last summer's game.

"My secret weapon."

"Seriously, where did he come from?"

"I brought him up from my farm team," Anderson had said.

Rick Allen had not appreciated the humor until now—and that was because the joke was on him.

He frowned and looked around the crowd. Soon enough he spotted a woman who had to be Billy's mother. She was a strong, tall, sandy-haired woman who clapped loudly and whistled with two fingers in her mouth; the father, a silent, dark-complected man wearing orange coveralls sat beside her. Rick Allen put away his notes and slowly worked his way through the crowd toward Billy's parents. With the right talk, the right moves, the joke might end up on Coach Anderson. More than a few kids from western Flint County went to Buckman High School. These things could be worked out, especially for a pitcher like Billy Baggs. . . .

But the best person to ask about the big game was Aaron Goldberg—Coach Goldberg. Right now he paced behind the Farm Team bench. It was the top of the fourth inning, Farm Team 2, Town Team 1—but threatening. One out and bases loaded, no thanks to two fly balls let drop in left field, and a walk. King Kenwood kicked dirt as he dug in at the plate.

"Time!" Aaron called, and walked to the mound.

"Now what?" Billy muttered as he stared at the runners surrounding him, then at King Kenwood.

"Forget about the runners," Aaron said. "Just

keep the ball down in the strike zone. High balls are fly balls—which we don't need."

"You can say that again," Billy said, glancing disgustedly at his outfield.

"Low balls are ground balls. Ground balls we can deal with."

"Straighten up that damn hay bale," Billy muttered, looking to home plate. "Kenwood's not even gonna see the ball."

"Don't overthrow," Goldberg warned. "Just good, low strikes, all right?"

"Okay, okay."

Goldberg trotted off, and Billy took the rubber. From the stretch position he eyed the runners, then fired low and hard. Kenwood bounced a foul sharply off the plate.

"Stee-rike one!" the sheriff called.

The next pitch came in dangerously high and fast, but King swung just underneath it. The ball went straight up very high, then curved backward and fell—*Plang!*—onto the roof of the corn-crib. There were sudden bird calls of alarm from the Lutheran women.

Billy smiled and felt himself relax some.

He stepped off the mound and rubbed up a new ball.

Kenwood stepped out of the box.

Then the two rivals faced each other again. Inside his glove Billy slightly altered his fastball grip. Usually he put two fingers, side by side, directly over the top and crossways to the seams.

It was the standard fastball grip that Coach Anderson had taught him. But Billy had experimented on his own, and found that by widening his long fingers, by getting more white space between them, he gave the ball a tendency to drop. He didn't know what the pitch was called, and he had never used it in a game situation. But at 0 and 2, he could afford to waste one.

He stared down at the hay bale and behind it, to the peeping right eye of Heather Erickson. She nodded and gave him the thumbs-up sign. Heather gave him the thumbs-up sign before every pitch; it was the only sign she used.

Billy nodded, reared back and threw. King, waiting for a fastball, timed it perfectly—but only topped the sharply dropping ball. The ball spun and died just in front of home plate.

"Get it!" Billy shouted to Heather.

Who did.

She pounced on it, dashed back to touch home plate, then fired to first base—in time to double up King Kenwood by half a step.

The Farm Team went wild! "That's the inning—way to go, Heather!" the boys shouted as they raced off the field. Behind the home-plate screen Suzy Langen clapped, too. King Kenwood cursed and kicked dirt all the way back to the bench. Heather shot a triumphant glance toward the fence and Dale Schwartz. Then, instead of joining her team in the dugout, she walked slowly toward the mound. Billy stopped to stare. Heather went straight to the mound and stepped onto it like it was a podium; she turned to stare at the crowd.

The Town Team, uncertain of what was going on, did not cross the white lines to take the field.

"Umpire's time," the sheriff called. Noise in the stands slowly died.

"I got something to say," Heather said, "and this is as good a time as any." At first her voice was soft.

The buzz of voices in the stands went away altogether. Even the old ladies in the corncrib stood still and peered out and listened.

"As you know, I had a baby a while ago." She looked down briefly, then back up.

People glanced at each other uncertainly, then turned back to Heather.

"So far I ain't given my baby a name," she continued.

There was absolute silence in the stands.

"Well, I finally decided on one," she said. "I'm going to call him Dale, after his father—Dale Schwartz." She pointed into the stands at Schwartz—whose eyes bugged out. Suddenly he was gone, oozing backward, disappearing through the crowd like a snake into tall grass. Moments later a car door slammed and an engine raced.

At home plate the sheriff squinted hard at Schwartz's yellow El Camino as it roared off. On the mound, Heather began to cry.

The sheriff came quickly forward. "Heather, I'm proud of you," he said. "After the game I need to have you answer some questions."

She nodded, wiping her dusty face with her arm.

"And then I'll be taking in Mr. Schwartz for a real long chat," he added as he led her off the field.

In the stands there was clapping, at first a single pair of hands. Billy turned. It was Mavis, standing up, clapping for Heather. Then, one by one, more and more people stood and began to clap. The whole scene ended in a standing ovation, with the Farm Team chanting, "Heather! Heather!"

"Okay—okay," the sheriff called, waving the Town Team onto the field. "We've got a game to finish."

As the Farm Team settled onto the bench for the bottom of the fourth inning, Aaron smiled at Billy. "By the way, what kind of pitch was that last one to Kenwood?"

Billy shrugged. "I call it my drop ball."

"I call it unhittable," Goldberg said happily. "I call it 'K all the way.'"

From across the field Coach Anderson called out to Billy, in a thanks-for-nothing tone, "Nice pitch!" His added comment was a sharp kick to the pine bench.

Billy grinned across at the coach, who was already strategizing with King Kenwood and Butch Redbird.

In the stands, after Billy's new pitch, Buckman coach Rick Allen made rapid notes on his little pad.

"What's that you're writing?" Billy heard his father say to Allen.

"Oh, it's nothing," Allen said quickly, with a brief laugh.

"I don't trust people who write things down on the sly," Abner growled.

Rick Allen smiled weakly.

"Don't mind him," Mavis said cheerfully. "He's been in jail."

The game remained a pitchers' duel. In the bottom of the sixth inning, Raúl González led off with a bunt single. Jesús sacrificed him to second. Mr. and Mrs. González cheered loudly in Spanish. The family seemed thinner and more weather-beaten each time they came for Friday-night baseball; Billy wondered how many acres of sugar beets they had hoed this very day.

Shawn moved Raúl to third with a fly out to right.

Billy focused himself for his at bat. He ran a deep count, stroking several long fouls. Then, like an idiot, he chased Kenwood's high heater and struck out. The score remained Farm Team 2, Town Team 1 as they went into the seventh and final inning.

Aaron Goldberg paced. He watched the sun dip lower and redder, its harsh light swinging itself directly toward home plate. There would be few if any more runs scored, he was certain of that. Not the way King and Billy were pitching. From here on out it was a defensive game. His big worry now was pitches up from Billy. Billy was tiring.

"You feel okay?" he said to Billy just before Billy headed out to take the mound.

"Sure," Billy said, looking behind to the stands. Mavis waved. Abner was gazing about at the droves of people. Actually Billy was looking, as he did each inning, not toward his parents but at Suzy Langen. He kept waiting to see if she had moved from behind home plate. If she had chosen one side of the field or the other.

"Keep the ball low," Aaron cautioned. "Three outs and we've got this game."

"Sure," Billy said. "No problem."

Billy fanned Dave Nelson and Ricky Jokela; then trouble brewed. King Kenwood stepped in. The crowd quieted. Billy threw hard, but Kenwood fouled off pitch after pitch, and finally there was a full count. King lofted the next pitch to deep center. And Owen McGinty, running like crazy, stepped in a gopher hole and went down head over tennis shoes. Gina Erickson got a late start backing him up, and the ball rolled all the way to the fence—and, in a great break for the Farm Team—skipped underneath and into the forest of cows' legs.

"Ground rule triple," the sheriff called, waving King back to third.

There were shouts of disbelief from the Town Team bench.

"The batter had not passed third base before the ball went out of play," the sheriff explained. But Mark Kenwood charged onto the field to argue, nose to nose, the sheriff's ruling.

"Fan on the field," the sheriff called to Coach Anderson.

"Come on, Mark—let it go," the coach urged.

But Mark Kenwood persisted. His face was red. "Just because this is cow-lot baseball, there's no reason why—"

"Second warning," the sheriff said, turning sideways to Mark Kenwood.

Coach Anderson trotted onto the field—but not in time to prevent Mark Kenwood from kicking gravel onto the sheriff's shoes.

Which was a mistake.

The sheriff slowly looked down as his good leather shoes. His now-dusty, gravel-coated good leather shoes. All in one motion he reached into his back pocket, pulled out his handcuffs, spun Mark Kenwood around and slapped on the silvery manacles.

"What! You can't do this!"

"Says who?" said Harvey Olson. "I'm not only the umpire here, I'm the damn sheriff."

There were loud laughs (and some boos) from the stands. But the sheriff was serious. He led Mark Kenwood across to his motor home and padlocked him to the bumper. Mark Kenwood continued shouting as the sheriff headed back to home plate.

Coach Goldberg had taken advantage of the commotion to check on Owen McGinty, who was being tended to by none other than Doctor Lloyd. "Nothing broken," the doctor said. "It looks like a bad sprain that could use some ice."

"Sorry, guys," McGinty groaned, holding his

ankle. There were tears in his eyes. Someone
went for ice.

"Now we got nobody to play middle field—"
Gina said.

"Center field!" Billy muttered.

"Yeah—what are we gonna do?" voices
clamored.

The Farm Team all looked at Coach Goldberg,
who was absorbed in examining his clipboard.
"Roster change," he called decisively across to the
umpire. "Skinner to center for McGinty."

Billy grinned.

"Skinner?" the sheriff asked, looking around
for a new player.

"Skinner," Coach Anderson muttered, and
kicked the pine bench.

Billy unleashed the old Labrador and began
to run with him to center field. The dog spun
excited circles around Billy as the crowd tittered
with laughter.

"Protest!" King Kenwood said suddenly.

"Reason?" Coach Goldberg queried.

"Ah . . . no dogs on the field."

"Why not?" Aaron Goldberg said.

"'Cause there's a rule. Somewhere."

"This is not a sanctioned Little League game."

"Well then, because . . . because he's not on the
roster." He turned to Coach Anderson. "Is he?"

Coach Anderson could only smile. "Tenth
player listed, Skinner. No last name."

There was clapping and laughter in the

stands. One voice, with its pure, clean notes of pleasure, stood out above the rest. Suzy Langen shouted, "Come on, Skinner! Let's go, Farm Team!"

"Play ball," the sheriff called. "The sun's disappearing fast."

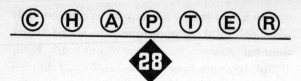

For some reason, perhaps because Suzy Langen now stood behind the Farm Team bench, perhaps because Skinner barked wildly from center field, perhaps because King Kenwood danced on third base—or likely a combination of all three—Billy could not find the strike zone. He walked Dusty Streeter on four pitches.

He went three and two on Jake Robertson, then bounced one into the hay bale for the second walk.

"Damn—" Billy muttered. The bases were loaded.

Aaron Goldberg came to the mound. "Shake it off. One more out and we've got the game. You can do it."

Billy nodded. He glanced toward Suzy Langen, then back to the plate. There Butch Redbird was about to dig in.

"Time," Coach Anderson called.

Butch looked over his shoulder.

"Pinch hitter," Coach Anderson said, and signaled to Tiny Tim Loren.

Butch was happy to step back; he and Billy were pals. But King Kenwood and his father went ballistic.

"Are you nuts, Coach?" Mark Kenwood shouted from the bumper of his motor home.

"Geez, Coach," King groaned, "we need a hitter in there."

"Are you sure, Coach?" Tiny Tim added, hanging back though holding a bat.

"Trust me," Coach Anderson said.

Tiny Tim, who had since last year improved a good deal as a hitter, stepped forward and dug in at the plate. He had a very small strike zone. Not only that, but Coach Anderson had some inside information. "Tim says you owe him one," he called to Billy with a grin.

Billy glared at the coach and at Tiny Tim.

"Is that true, Billy?" Coach Anderson needled.

"Maybe. Maybe not," Billy muttered, turning his back on Coach Anderson. He rubbed up the ball.

If there was a fat pitch, it was certainly not Billy's first one. A smoking fastball scorched the inside corner—Tim waved at it.

Pitch number two was another heater, which Tiny Tim managed to foul straight back.

"Okay, Billy, one more smoker," Aaron Goldberg shouted.

"Throw the jalapeño," the González brothers chattered.

The crowd was on its feet.

Billy swallowed. A promise was a promise, even to a pest like Tiny Tim. With the count at 0 and 2, he might as well get it over with.

On the third pitch Billy grooved a floater. Tiny Tim, crouched and waiting, whacked the ball to center field. He stood as stunned as Billy as the ball arced high and deep for certain extra bases. The whole Farm Team stood paralyzed.

"Fetch—" Billy screamed.

Skinner bolted from his set position. Tracking the ball all the way, he scrambled toward deep center field like a fighter plane scrambled for an intercept mission. To Billy, to the crowd, and to Tiny Tim, the action turned to slow motion.

Skinner taking longer and longer strides . . .

The ball carrying and carrying . . .

Skinner's legs eating up the ground . . .

The ball beginning to settle toward the fence . . .

Skinner's pink tongue flapping and flapping, pulling him, like a helicopter's propeller, off the ground . . .

The ball and Skinner angling in perfect timing toward each other—and to the roar of the crowd, Skinner snatching the ball from midair, then tumbling end over end on the ground and into the fence itself.

There was a sucking in of breath. Had Skinner held the ball?

Sheriff Olson, who had raced to second base to make the call, shaded his eyes.

Skinner got up, tail toward home plate, and

shook himself groggily—but when he turned, everyone could see the white sphere in his mouth.

"Out!" the sheriff called.

And the Farm Team went crazy.

Afterward there was laughing and dust and cars heading off down the road. First to leave, of course, was the motor home with the Town Team. But Coach Anderson stayed behind; he had spotted Rick Allen standing with Mavis and Abner Baggs—and right now the two coaches were having words behind the corncrib.

Suzy Langen lingered behind, too. She petted Skinner and fed him leftover brownies, all he could eat, but the old dog was sleepy now, and couldn't swallow another bite or keep his eyes open another second. The Farm Team laughed and kept passing the Kool-Aid pitcher.

Watching Suzy's long, smooth arms stroke Skinner's back, Billy could not recall having played baseball recently. He was floating a mile above cloud nine. Suzy looked up at him. "This was really fun, Billy. Will you have more games?"

"I . . ." Billy began.

Abner Baggs brought Billy crashing back to ground level. "Maybe we will, maybe we won't," he said sternly from a few paces away. Abner had clearly recovered most of his naturally bad humor, which was a relief to everyone. "Nice job on the mound," he added briefly, and came forward and shook hands with Billy. Billy grinned and held on to his dad's hand for a long time. For one insane moment he considered introducing Suzy Langen to his father, but recovered his senses at the last second.

The sheriff shouldered through the crowd. "Damn good coaching, too," he said to Aaron Goldberg. He was about to say more, but there were louder and louder words, now, from behind the corncrib. Suddenly Buckman Coach Rick Allen came flying forward and tumbled in the dust. "Excuse me," the sheriff said, turning away. "Looks like I've got some more umpiring to do."

On the field the victory party continued. Mavis went for her camera. Aaron Goldberg's parents, beaming, came forward to lock their son in a double-arm squeeze. "My son, the coach!" Rita Goldberg said proudly.

"Everybody on the Farm Team, let's get in here for a photo," Mavis called.

And they did. With dust and sunlight and cows and the crowd in the background, here's how the team lined up.

First row (sleeping): Skinner.
Second row, kneeling, from left: Jesús González, Heather Erickson (with baby Dale), Raúl González (with Juan Elvis González), Shawn Howenstein (on motorbike).
Third row: Danny Boyer, Aaron Goldberg, Owen McGinty, Bob McGinty, Billy Baggs.

• • •

That winter Billy would spend plenty of time looking at the photo. Suzy Langen was visible; clearly she was smiling at Billy. And if he held the photograph just so, behind the team, looking over Billy's right shoulder, there seemed to be one more player. His body and face were formed from the glow of sunlight and dust; from the curving white-and-black markings of the cows; from the clouds. It was Robert. And he was smiling.

Right now, however, as the Farm Team waited for Mavis to adjust her camera and to say "Say cheese," Aaron Goldberg turned to Billy. "I was wrong before," he said seriously. "*This* is the happiest moment of my life."

They were all laughing like crazy when the flashbulb went off.